The Dating Game

By B. N. Hale

27 Dates: The Series

The Dating Challenge

The Dating Secret

The Dating Game

The Christmas Date

The Valentine's Date

Table of Contents

Volume 14: The Falling Date

Chapter 1

"Yes."

Silence greeted Reed's answer and he could almost see the man's doubtful expression, even through the blindfold. He smiled, knowing the man probably thought him crazy, but nodded in an attempt to reassure him.

"Are you sure?" the man asked. "You're about to—"

"Don't tell him," Kate protested for the hundredth time. "You'll ruin the surprise."

"You really trust your girl this much?" the man asked, dubious. "To sign a waiver with no idea what you're signing?"

"Yes," he said. "Now can we get on with it?"

Someone behind them called out. "Just let him sign already!"

The man blew out his breath and muttered to himself, and a moment later a pen was shoved into Reed's hand. Kate caught his hand and directed him where to sign, and he scribbled his name. Then she led him out of the line.

Reed stumbled as his foot caught and he almost reached up to remove the blindfold. His girlfriend—a term he was still getting used to using—had asked him to put it on a mile before they arrived at their destination, and he had no idea what lay in store.

They were outside, but that was all he knew. Under the August sun, sweat trickled down his neck, the Colorado heat baking his skin through his shorts and t-shirt. His vision was blocked, but he could make out shapes.

They were in a small crowd of people. Some laughed and talked, and a young man whined, impatiently waiting for his turn. Reed smelled cotton candy and corn dogs, and would have thought it was a fair if there had been carnival music. Instead there was only the hot wind and a faint crashing of water. Then Kate brought him to a halt.

"I didn't expect him to be so resistant," she said, lowering her voice. "It's not like you were signing your life away."

"I wouldn't know," he said.

Kate's hand touched his, her soft fingers threading into his own. He smiled, pleased to find that even after two weeks, the power of her touch had yet to diminish. Her lips brushed against his, commanding his attention until she retreated.

"I can't believe you're doing this," she said, her voice a shade uncertain. "You really trust me this much?"

"It was your turn to plan the date," he said.

There was a distant click, and then voices screamed, the sound mounting as they approached and then sped away. The terror of the screamers was evident, but a moment later laughter mingled with the fear.

He grinned as he listened to what he could only assume lay in store for him. "Just remember that whatever you do to me, I get to do to you."

"Perhaps I've gone too far," Kate said with a laugh.

"Can't back out now," Reed protested. "I want free reign on our next date."

"Are you sure?" she asked.

"I may be new to the whole boyfriend thing," he said, "but isn't trust a prerequisite?"

"Trust, yes," she said. "But this is a *lot* of trust."

Reed's arm was still around her back from the previous kiss, so he pulled her close. "Your invite mentioned something about falling for each other? How can I refuse that?"

Her smile was evident in her tone. "The falling part is easy," she said. "I promise."

He smiled, and pictured her in his mind. Her dark hair hung about her shoulders, her green eyes sparkling. She was beautiful and witty, her subtle courage— a power that had almost been hidden when they'd first met—seeming to grow with every date.

"What's that smile for?"

"Just thinking about how all this started," he said.

"The blondes set us up on a blind date," she said, "on Valentine's Day."

He grinned at her nickname for her three roommates—only one of whom was actually blonde. Reed had gotten to know the trio of girls over the last few months and found them to be smart, loyal, and on occasion, devious.

"Does that mean they get credit for bringing us together?" he asked.

She snorted and shook her head, the motion just visible through the blindfold. "*I* get the credit. They set us up, but I'm the one who issued the challenge."

"You think *you* deserve the credit?" he teased. "It was my date that made you want to ask me out in the first place."

"Perhaps you get *some* credit," she allowed.

He leaned in and took her hand, wishing he could see her expression. "You deserve the credit," he said softly. "Without you, we never would have come this far."

"We both had a past to resolve," she said. "I had Jason and you had Aura."

He thought of Aura, the girl he'd once loved. Her accident was still seared into his memory, her voice on the phone, fading, as he waited the agonizing minutes for the ambulance to arrive. Yet Kate had helped heal the open wound of that moment, and the scar had finally faded.

"And now we have each other," Reed said.

"That we do," she said, leaning up to kiss him again.

Six months ago, the dating challenge had started out as a game, but they had brought their challenge to culmination in their date at the Festival of Lanterns, where he'd finally kissed her beneath a celestial tapestry of floating lights. Even after two weeks, every kiss sent lightning through his body, robbing him of breath and scattering his thoughts. The contact was temporary, the impact was lasting.

"It's not fair that your kisses do that to me," he said.

"You hadn't kissed a girl in three years," she said. "Kissing *any* girl would have been powerful."

He was holding her hand, so he used the contact to pull her in, trapping her in his arms. "Only you," he said softly.

She made no move to escape. "Is that why you agreed to be blindfolded? Because I kissed you?"

"It's possible," he admitted.

She leaned up, her lips caressing his, a tease that revealed her smile. "I like having this power," she said with a laugh.

Once again the click echoed and the crowd hushed as another three voices expressed their terror, the sound rising and falling before returning again. He turned toward the sound. By this point he was confident Kate had brought him to a ride, probably a giant swing. The prospect of doing it with a blindfold instilled a spark of nervousness.

"It's our first challenge date as a real couple," he said. "So you've decided to test my limits? Isn't that for the third date?"

"We passed the third date months ago," she said.

"We hadn't even held hands," he said, recalling the St. Patrick's Date.

"True," she said. "But we both know what we felt."

"Then why the blindfold?" He motioned to the cloth tied over his face.

"Actually, this was Ember's idea," she said.

"Of course it was," Reed said with a sigh.

Reed liked Ember, but he knew that if the diminutive redhead ever fought a marine, it would be the marine that went home crying for his mother. Despite her temper, Ember's loyalty to her friends could not be questioned, and Reed counted himself lucky to call her one of his own.

"Reed Thompson and Kate Williams!" a voice called. "You're next!"

"It's our turn," Kate said.

Her voice was bright but shaky. If she felt nervous—when she had the advantage of seeing what was coming—how much more should he be afraid? Her hand caught his elbow and guided him forward.

"Are you ready?" she asked.

"For what?"

She laughed, sounding amused and a little afraid. "Isn't it obvious? I want you to fall for me."

Chapter 2

"Your invite said nothing about fear," Reed said.

"I talked about falling," she said. "The fear was implied."

The blindfold had shifted and he could see his feet as two unseen women strapped him into a harness. The sheer volume of buckles and safety straps was alarming enough, but then they were walked out onto a stretch of stone and he heard metal clicking into place where the harness bound them together.

"You did say you're not afraid of heights," she said.

"Flyers ready!" someone shouted.

The cable on their back began to shift, and he released a nervous laugh. "It's entirely different when you're blindfolded—"

He sucked in his breath as the cord on his back went taut, lifting them off the platform. Already holding her hand, he tightened his grip like Kate was a lifeline. She laughed at his tension, but it betrayed her own rising fear.

"We're obviously going up," he said, raising his voice over the wind. "But how high?"

"You'll know when you take off the blindfold," she said. "But I want you to wait until we get to the top."

"This is absolutely terrifying," he exclaimed. "So forgive me if I scream like a little girl."

She gasped. "In a moment I think we'll both be screaming."

"Don't say that!" he shouted. "I don't even know what's beneath us!"

"I know!" she laughed. "That's what makes this fun!"

"For you or me?"

"Me!"

He laughed, terrified and excited all at once. They continued to rise, the air buffeting them in the ascent. The blindfold had shifted again and he caught glimpses of metal girders and a crowd of people.

As their movement came to an abrupt halt, he emitted a very unmanly squeak. They swung for a moment and he clenched her hand, her grip as tight as his. He swallowed repeatedly and fought to breathe.

"You can remove the blindfold, now," she called.

"I'm not sure I want to!"

She laughed and reached up with her free hand, pulling the blindfold from his head. He squinted at the sudden brilliance. Then his eyes adjusted and his stomach sought to eject from his body.

They were a hundred feet off the ground, with only thin cables holding them aloft. Two sets of cables extended from the anchor points on their back. One held them in place, while the other extended up and away, connecting to a great arch that overlooked a plunging canyon.

He'd thought it was going to be a giant swing, but not one this big. They hung suspended high above the earth, but the swing would take them over a plunging canyon. Never in his life had he felt such fear, and he clung to Kate.

"*Flyers ready!*" a voice boomed over a loudspeaker.

"Reed," she said.

"I'm okay," he blurted, and again, "I'm okay—wow we're high."

"*Reed*," she said, more urgently than before.

He tore his eyes from the endless vista to meet her gaze. Her eyes were arresting in their intensity. Her lips were pulled into a tight smile, a touch of mischief mingled with fear and excitement.

"Will you fall for me?"

He laughed lightly. "I don't think I have much choice now!"

She grinned. "Exactly."

"*Three!*" the voice boomed.

Surrounded by open air and terror, he still had her at his side, the solitude making their proximity all the more intimate. Her eyes were filled with courage and excitement, an invitation to join her in what was to come.

"*Two!*"

She smiled and squeezed his hand, reminding him of the first time he'd held hers. He'd never felt such a bond as when their fingers intertwined. He smiled in turn.

"*One!*"

He swallowed and clung tighter. "I'm afraid it's too late," he said. "I already fell for you."

Her expression brightened and she grasped the handle at the side of her waist. Their hands turned white as they held on and she glanced his way for a final approval. Then she yanked and the cord at their back released.

For an instant they hovered in space, as if gravity was unprepared for their sudden freedom. The harness drifted away from Reed's chest and he held it with his free hand, desperate to feel connected. Then gravity reached up and yanked them toward the earth.

The shout ripped from his lips as they accelerated. The second cable snapped taut and they bounced into the curve, the force pushing them into the harness. He watched the earth approach at frightening speed, the people in the crowd blurring as they reached the base of the swing. Then abruptly the ground dropped away and they swung out over the canyon.

The gorge plunged into the earth, a distant view of water crashing in its depths. If the cord snapped, he would have several horror-filled moments before death, and he braced for the sound of snapping cables that did not come.

They slowed as the arc reached its pinnacle, their sheer height inspiring renewed fear. Kate's hair floated upward and framed her face, and they shared a look, their grins wild and terrified and excited.

They began to fall again, only this time it seemed they were plummeting into the canyon. Their matching yells rose in pitch as they hurtled toward the base of the swing, the gigantic curve carrying them back over the edge of the canyon before arcing high once more.

Reed began to laugh, the caged fear and delight gushing in amusement. Kate laughed at his side, the sound tinged with fear and awe. As they passed over the canyon again he managed to extend his arms outward, flying up the arc.

"This is incredible!" he shouted over the rushing wind.

"I can't believe you trusted me!" she shouted back.

Her voice carried a touch of surprise. "Did you really think I'd refuse?" he asked.

"Maybe." She smiled and put her arms out as they swung upward again. "Maybe I wanted to see what kind of boyfriend you would be."

"Did I pass the test?"

"With flying colors," she said brightly.

"So no more tests?" he asked.

"No promises," she said mischievously.

She shifted in the harness and leaned closer but couldn't close the gap on her own. He tilted his head, kissing her as they flew out over the canyon. The exhilaration of the swing added to the kiss, making it all the more intense.

She pulled back, her smile positively wicked. "Let's see how far I can push you."

"Just remember my turn is next," he warned.

"I know," she replied, and her expression turned challenging. "Feel free to push any boundaries you'd like."

She'd called his bluff and he laughed. "And I thought swings were safe."

She grinned and spread her arms wide as they swung a slow circle. "Don't worry," she said. "I know exactly what do with you on the playground."

"Will it require a blindfold?" he asked. "Because tag is not very fun when one person is blindfolded."

"We played tag for six months," she said, "and as you said, I already caught you."

"So finder's keepers?"

She burst into a laugh, the sound echoing into the gorge as they flew over it again. The swing had slowed, each arc lower than before. The initial terror had been replaced by a flurry of apprehension each time they soared over the ravine, and Reed marveled at the river far below.

White water crashed over boulders and stones, the stony crags deepening as the stream carved its way east. The canyon was not overly large, but viewed from above with nothing but a slim harness holding them aloft, it seemed much more impressive.

He squeezed Kate's hand, marveling at how she could look so stunning with her hair billowing about her face. She fought the gust until she'd tamed her hair and then noticed Reed's expression.

"What?" she asked.

"I hated the blindfold," he said.

"Really?" she asked, her expression disappointed. "I'm sorry—"

"I prefer to see what I'm falling for."

"Very smooth."

"What?" he asked. "I thought was nice."

"It was," she admitted, and leaned over to kiss him. "And I like seeing you too."

"So no more blindfolds?"

"Deal," she said, and then grinned. "But that doesn't mean I can't push you."

Chapter 3

The swing gradually slowed until an employee was able to snag them. He unhooked them from the cable and then began the complicated process of removing the safety harness. As he helped Reed to his feet he shook his head in disbelief.

"I can't believe you went up blindfolded," he said. "Never had anyone do that before. Was it a dare?"

"More like a challenge," Reed said, stepping free of the harness.

"Who's winning?" he asked.

Reed and Kate exchanged a look and said in unison. "Me."

They laughed and exited the ride, making their way past the line to the parking lot. She'd had Reed don the blindfold a mile before they arrived, so it was the first time he had a chance to look around. As they left, he looked up at the sign.

"The Royal Gorge Skycoaster," he read aloud. "The highest skycoaster in the world." He looked to Kate with a wry smile. "You should try it blind."

"I think I'll leave that to you," she said.

"Once was enough," he said fervently.

They walked to the car and she opened the door for him. Now that they were dating officially he'd argued that he should get to open her door but she'd been insistent. When it was her turn in the dating challenge, she got to be in charge.

"Are we going straight back?" he asked.

It had been nearly a three hour drive down from Boulder, but it had seemed much shorter. Being with Kate had changed his entire outlook on life, and time was never enough. He recognized that such an emotion could not last, but for now, he did not want to acknowledge the spark of worry.

"Not yet," she said. "We have one more thing to do."

"Really?" he asked.

"Do you mind if we eat while we drive?" she asked, pulling out her phone to check the time. "The line at the skycoaster took longer than I thought, so we're running a little behind."

He reached to the bag she'd stashed in the back and withdrew the sandwiches they'd picked up before leaving Boulder. As they ate she drove northeast, heading back the way they had come, with Reed adeptly feeding them both.

"Drink," she said.

He lifted her cup so she could sip from the straw, allowing her to keep one hand on the wheel. She smiled and nodded her gratitude and then took another bite of the sandwich. They'd picked up Subway and he'd been surprised by her order. She didn't usually get spicier food.

"How's your Spicy Italian?" he asked.

"Flavorful," she said, the word muffled through the food in her mouth.

He grinned and took a bite of his own sandwich. "I have to admit something," he said.

She took a bite and cast him a curious look. "What?"

"I kind of wish we'd started dating like this sooner."

"Really?" she asked, her lips twitching into a smile. "Why?"

"I missed six months with you," he said.

19

"We both had some things to work through."

"Sorry it took so long," he said.

"I'm not," she said. "For most couples, the honeymoon phase of a relationship lasts a few weeks. For us it lasted six months—apart from when we broke up."

"We weren't actually dating," he said, "so I'm not sure we can call it a break up."

"That's what my roommates called it, so that's what I call it." She tipped her sandwich to him. "But right now I can't stop thinking of the last few weeks, and how much fun it's been to be together."

"How long does the honeymoon phase usually last?" he asked, his previous thought returning.

"I keep forgetting you've never had a serious relationship," she said. "You're already so good at the boyfriend thing."

"I'm still in training, remember?"

"I remember," she said, pulling onto the freeway.

He laughed at her expression. Over the last few days they'd started a game called "does a boyfriend do." He'd cooked her breakfast and surprised her at work, much to Kate's obvious delight.

"Does a boyfriend kiss a girl while she drives?" she asked.

"No he does not," he said. He reached out and kissed the back of her hand. "At least not on the lips."

She grinned and took another bite. Then she sped up to pass a minivan doing sixty on the freeway. Reed watched the woman yell at her kids as they drove by, wondering if she realized they were going so slow. Her husband was in the passenger seat, his attention on his phone. It made Reed wonder if ten years ago, the couple had been driving on the same road before they'd gotten married, their whole life ahead of them.

Had they too, felt that time was never enough? Surely the initial euphoria of a new relationship had faded, but they'd overcome the ensuing conflicts to get married and have a family. It made Reed wonder what lay ahead for them.

"Why do you think the honeymoon phase ends?" he asked.

She shrugged. "I think it's just time. At first you are discovering everything about each other, the quirks, the habits, the things that make you unique. It's wonderful. Then one day you realize your boyfriend isn't as attractive as he was on the night you went drinking, or he says something that used to be funny but suddenly isn't. Or maybe you begin to fight and the attractions just fades."

"Is that going to happen to us?"

"No," she said, glancing his way, her eyes traveling up and down his body as a hint of a smile appeared on her lips. "I think we would have hit that point months ago."

"So what *is* going to happen to us?"

She asked for another bite and he waited for her answer. He'd thought the question before, but been afraid to ask, afraid to shatter the wonder of their new relationship. But now it seemed the question wanted its own answer.

"We can't always want the same thing," she said.

"Is that what happened to you and Jason?" he asked.

She nodded and took the last bite of her sandwich. Then she crumpled the wrapper and dropped it into the bag at Reed's feet. Picking up her cup, she swallowed and then gestured vaguely south, toward Arizona and her youth.

"Three weeks," she said. "That's how long Jason and I were together before the first incident."

"The first?" he asked.

21

"He had a soccer game the same night I was supposed to have a choir rehearsal. It wasn't mandatory but it felt like it was. I told him I couldn't go to his game and he wasn't happy."

"Just a game?"

"The championship," she said. "They lost and I wasn't there. He blamed me."

"Really?"

She nodded. "It seems so juvenile as I say it, but we got into our first fight because of that."

"Well, I don't have an upcoming game, so I think we're safe."

"For now," she said with a smile. "But remember, things come up. A relationship is strong because of what it endures, not because of the depth of the feelings."

"I am but the apprentice," he said.

The conversation shifted, but throughout the drive Reed found his thoughts returning to her warning. She'd said it in amusement, but he sensed an element of seriousness to the words, and wondered what the source of their first conflict as a real couple would be.

His thoughts were interrupted when they got off the exit for Cheyenne Mountain. Refusing his request for a destination, she drove into the mountains, threading her way higher and higher until they were surrounded by trees and the road had turned to gravel.

Sunlight streamed through the canopy to illuminate the road, the warm summer air pulling at the leaves. The forest grew denser as they drove until she pulled off the road and parked at a tiny, nearly invisible trailhead. Reed exited the car and breathed deep.

"This is beautiful," he said. "Where are we?"

She popped the trunk and grabbed two backpacks. "The Titan Falls Trailhead."

22

"Never heard of it."

"It's not one of the popular hiking spots," she said, handing him a backpack.

"How'd you learn of it?"

"Before I answer that, I have a question for you."

He turned at her somber tone. "What's wrong?"

"Does a boyfriend help his girlfriend replace bad memories?"

Kate's expression was tight, lines of worry creasing her forehead. Reed sensed the weight to her question, and realized that, just by asking it, she was showing a vulnerability she had never revealed before. He stepped in and wrapped his arms around her waist. Then he brushed a hair out of her face and marveled at the profound sense of unity.

"Yes, he does."

She smiled, but the expression betrayed a trace of nervousness. "This way," she said. "It's a half hour hike."

Curious, he followed her into the woods. She accepted his hand and began, "About a year before he proposed, Jason took me here. He wanted to plan something special but the weather didn't cooperate."

"Rookie mistake," he lamented. "You have to check the weather."

She smiled faintly. "He brought a picnic and a blanket so we could be alone at the falls."

"And it didn't work out?"

"It started to rain. He got frustrated and we argued, and the fight lasted for hours. This place was so magical I wanted to come back, but the memory seemed spoiled, and we never returned."

"And now you're bringing me?"

"Do you mind that it's something from my time with Jason?" she asked.

Her expression betrayed her nervousness, and a trace of regret. Whatever lay ahead, she'd regretted it for years, and now hoped he could erase the burden. He smiled and squeezed her hand.

"I can't wait."

She smiled, and she picked up the pace. Shortly after, they broke through the trees and a small creek came into view. It gurgled past rocks and into swirling eddies before disappearing over a cliff. They approached the edge and he gazed down on a hidden grotto in the mountains.

"Welcome to Titan Falls," she said.

Chapter 4

Reed gazed upon the secret refuge in awe. The stream dropped off the cliff and cascaded into a pool of water. Surrounded by trees and rocks, the clear pond flowed into a stream that disappeared into the forest. Sunlight pierced through the canopy and plunged into the pond, illuminating the depths.

A trail led to the base of the falls, winding down a steep switchback before reaching the pond in the base of the grotto. The waterfall struck the water, sending mist coalescing on trees and rocks, the moisture permeating the air like magic.

"This is stunning," Reed said. He turned to find Kate removing her shirt.

She motioned to the water with a smile of anticipation. "You want to go swimming, don't you?"

She reached for her undershirt and his face burned red. He quickly turned away, his response causing her to laugh. The sound came out muffled from the shirt passing over her head. Facing the trees, he swallowed and shifted his feet, struggling to speak.

"Relax," she called, her voice farther away. "I'm behind a tree. Your swimsuit is in your backpack. I had Jackson pack it with a towel."

Snagging the bag and resisting the urge to sneak a look, he ducked behind a tree to change. He also found a pair of water shoes which came from his roommate. Jackson was four inches taller and the shoes were too big, but wearing them was better than walking around barefoot. When he returned he found her in a cute suit with straps threaded across the back and sides.

"You could have warned me," he said.

She grinned mischievously. "I know your position on sex." She leaned up and kissed him. "But that doesn't mean I can't tease you."

"You enjoy this far too much," he grumbled.

She grinned and caught his hand, pulling him toward the top of the waterfall. At twenty feet high it wasn't enormous, but it was high enough to inspire fear. The light allowed Reed to see the depth and clarity of the pond.

"Ready?" she asked, her eyes bright with excitement.

"At least I'm not blindfolded."

They took a step to the edge and leapt, the wind rushing over them as they fell and plunged into the pond. Unprepared for the cold, Reed instinctively swam to the surface and sucked in a breath. Kate breached the water next to him and cried out in delight. Her dark hair lay down her back, the water glistening on her face.

"It's freezing!" she gasped.

"I think you mean refreshing," he said.

He swam to a section where the water spun in the sunlight long enough to be warmed. Although the wind still carried a chill, the spot was significantly warmer than where they'd landed.

He splashed her as she neared and she gasped, and then splashed him back. For several furious moments they batted water at each other, their shouts echoing off the stone walls adjacent to the waterfall.

When they tired, they climbed the trail back to the waterfall. It was steep, but they used roots and branches, the wood rough on his wet palms as he helped push Kate higher up the trail, privately admiring her figure.

When they reached the top they jumped again, and this time the water lacked its previous chill. Another water fight ensued, with both splashing and shoving each other into the colder sections of the pond. The fight came to an end when he caught her hand and pulled her close.

"How long have you wanted to jump off a waterfall?" he asked.

"Since I was a teenager," she admitted, wiping the water from her face. "My friend's first kiss was in a pond like this one. She said it was magical, and I was quite envious."

"You want to kiss beneath the waterfall?" he used his chin to point to the cascade.

"I thought you'd never ask," she said.

They swam to the waterfall, to a shallow curve of rock behind the cascade. Wreathed in mist, Kate seemed to glow, the sunlight piercing the waterfall and striking the water on her bare shoulders.

He wrapped an arm around her back. Supremely conscious of the thin layer of material that separated their bodies, he brushed his fingers across her bare back, swallowing as the contact elicited a surge of desire.

She held his gaze, shuddering at his touch. Her lips were cold and trembling, but quickly heated from the passion of the kiss. Her arms tightened around his neck, binding them together, the mist swirling about their shoulders.

When they parted she spoke as if afraid to disturb the magic of the alcove. "I dare say the movies fail to capture the moment."

Reed swallowed, his mouth abruptly dry. "You never came down here with Jason?"

She shook her head, her fingers playing with his back. "The rain stopped us, remember?"

"I've never been so grateful for a rainy day."

She laughed and tilted her head back, her eyes holding him bound, an invitation which he accepted. The second kiss was no less powerful than the first, leaving them both breathless. He was highly aware of her sleek curves that pressed against him, of her trembling from the chill.

"Care to warm up?" he asked.

"I think I just did," she said. She smiled and then acquiesced with a nod.

They dived through the waterfall together and swam to the shore, where they climbed onto a boulder in the sun. They both smiled as the heat of the boulder seeped into their backs, and settled in to warm up.

Kate sighed. "Do you remember the mountains of our first date?"

"How could I forget?"

"On that night I remembered this place," she said, sweeping her hand at the grotto. "Because of you I realized I didn't have to wait for a guy to bring me here, that I could ask a guy out myself."

"And you chose to bring me?"

"I didn't think that then," she said. "But I did later. When our dating challenge became more serious I wondered if I could bring you. I didn't, of course, but only because I wasn't sure how you'd react knowing I had been here with Jason."

"What was that day like?" he asked, dipping his feet into the water.

"It was overcast and the rain made water even colder," she said. "I didn't want to jump off the waterfall, so he did alone, and came out shaking. He was furious and frustrated and we argued about whether the rain would stop. Eventually we returned to the car and tried to wait out the rain. I think he was mad because he wanted it to be special and it was a colossal failure."

"Did he often ask you on dates like this?" he asked.

"Rarely," she said. "Like I told you, he was too busy. I think that's why he was so upset when it didn't work out. He blamed himself."

"I once took a girl to an aquarium," he said. "She was studying to be a biologist and loved that kind of thing. The place was huge and had a "Dive Into the Deep" program, where you could scuba dive with the animals."

"Sounds like a perfect date," she said.

"It was. Except I didn't check when it was going to be open."

She winced. "It was closed?"

"For renovations," he replied. "I had driven us an hour and a half to get there. We ate at a tiny diner and then drove home." He chuckled in chagrin. "I hadn't been doing the creative dating very long."

"Ouch," she said. "How did she take it?"

"She told me it was the thought that counts," he said. "But it was clear she was disappointed. I couldn't blame her. I'd talked it up for most of the drive."

She blinked in surprise. "I just realized. We never played the Worst Date Game."

"I think we're talking about bad dates now," he said.

She grinned, her eyes sparkling with mischief. "Maybe. But when it's my turn, I'm doing that game for real."

"Deal," he said. "Because we never got around to playing one of my favorite games."

"Which is?"

He shook his head and smiled. "You'll find out when it's my turn."

She frowned and flicked lingering water at him, but the water had warmed in the sun so he suggested they jump in again. For the next hour they took turns swimming, talking, and jumping into the pond. They talked and kissed until the cold seeped into their skin and they played anew, and Reed relished the sense of solitude and closeness.

He'd often wondered what dating for real would be like. Now as they cavorted about in a secret grotto, he realized he could not have anticipated how wondrous it could be—especially with a woman like Kate.

When her attention was elsewhere, he stole glances—at her figure, her features, but mostly her eyes. There was an air of peace about her, as if she were finally unfettered. She caught him looking but merely smiled as if daring him to keep looking, and he sensed a hint of danger.

The freedom inspired by the grotto was limited by the physical boundaries he'd placed on their relationship. It had taken them months to just hold hands, and he guessed she was wondering how long it would take for him to be comfortable with more. She did not push him, but in each kiss he sensed her desire.

When the sun had descended behind the trees, the temperature dropped and they reluctantly left the pond. They took a picture so the waterfall was visible in the background, continuing the tradition from their earlier dates. The lights shined off the white cascade, illuminating the background and almost capturing the magic of the refuge. Then they slowly gathered their things and departed. Reed cast a final look before the trail took the grotto from view.

"Promise we can come back?" he asked.

"Of course," she said. "There's still something I'd like to do here."

Her laugh was devilish as she turned and strode away, leaving him to imagine what she meant. He shook his head as he watched her go. They'd been together for just a short time but he was shocked at the depth of his attraction to Kate.

"What have I gotten myself into," he murmured.

"Try to keep up," she called, glancing over her shoulder with a coy smile.

He grinned and hurried to join her, taking her hand as they walked the trail back to her car. The trees were no less magical than the grotto, and the trail ascended through a forest lit by a descending sun. They reached the trailhead and got into her car. They'd been at the grotto for several hours and the sun had begun to set, the sky darkening to red and orange as they descended the mountain.

"Today's been perfect, you know that?"

She nodded in agreement and reached out for his hand. "A perfect day," she repeated. "I look forward to many more."

He smiled and looked out the window at the sun, his thoughts turning to their earlier conversation about an approaching conflict. After such a day he couldn't imagine what would set them against each other, but the descending darkness left him wondering how much longer they could push back the clock before life sought to pull them apart.

Chapter 5

They drove home, laughing and talking about the waterfall and the skycoaster. For the first time since they'd started the dating challenge, he felt out of his depth. Kate had learned from his methods about dating, but he was just starting to understand what it meant to be a boyfriend. When he said as much, she smiled.

"You really feel that way?" she asked, glancing his way.

"I do," he admitted. "Because of how much time is required, planning a creative date implies a deeper connection. I was always careful to avoid dates that would be too intimate. With you, I *want* to do that, but I don't have a lot of ideas."

She cast him a suspicious look. "Are you just trying to throw me off track?"

"Not at all," he said. "Today has been perfect, and I wonder if I can plan dates that live up to the same level."

"You're not about to quit, are you?"

"Of course not," he said. "But I thought that's what boyfriends do—they express their fears."

"Now you're afraid of me?" she asked, her lips twitching with amusement.

"You can be intimidating," he said with a smile. "After Ember posts this to her blog and tells of the waterfall date, I suspect public favor will swing in your direction. I'm just feeling the pressure to come up with the next event."

"I'm confident you can deliver," she said. "But the day isn't over yet."

He raised an eyebrow. "Don't tell me there's more."

"You'll have to wait and find out," she said.

He issued a self-deprecating laugh. "What exactly are you trying to prove? Today has already been perfect."

"I've wanted to date like this for months," she hesitated, and then added, "now that we are, I find a surprising sense of worry."

"About what?" he asked.

She glanced his way and then returned her attention to the road. "You've been doing your creative dating for three years and never dated seriously. Part of me is worried that you'll get tired of dating just one girl."

"That's not going to happen."

"How can you be sure?" she asked. "The last two weeks have been incredible—beyond incredible, actually—but how can I know you'll want to stay with me?"

"Because I *really* like dating you," he said. "And I don't want to stop." He was already holding her hand so he squeezed it. "You have nothing to worry about."

"Maybe I went a bit overboard today," she admitted.

"Not at all," he said. "I just assumed you wanted to set the bar so high I could never beat it."

"That too."

He snorted a laugh as they got off the exit in Boulder. They drove through town until they got to his house, where they'd left that morning after breakfast together. It was getting dark, and he realized it was the first time in years that he'd ever spent the entire day with a girl.

They pulled into his driveway and got out. Although they'd walked to the door together many times since the beginning of their dating challenge, today felt different. She seemed to feel it as well and betrayed a touch of nervousness as she stood on his doorstep.

"I can't tell you how many times I wanted to kiss you after a date," she said.

"Hugs were just not enough," he agreed.

She grinned and leaned into a kiss, but the door opened and Jackson stood framed in the doorway.

Tall and muscular, Reed's roommate wore a t-shirt that said, *Should be supervised at all times*. He loved every sport, and usually played with his girlfriend Shelby. He folded his arms and looked on in disapproval.

"Do you have any idea how late it is?"

"Seven?" Reed asked, confused.

Jackson scowled. "I've been slaving over dinner for hours, and you didn't have the decency to call?"

Kate groaned. "I'm sorry Jackson. I got caught up with things today and forgot to tell you we were running late."

"Call about what?" Reed asked.

"I promised Jackson and Shelby we would join them for dinner when we got back," Kate said, and then turned to Jackson. "I didn't realize it would take so long."

"It doesn't matter," Jackson said, uncharacteristically grumpy.

Shelby appeared next to him. Also tall and blonde, she had the lithe figure of an athlete, and wore a shirt for her favorite team, the Lakers. She caught Jackson's hand, pulling him out of the doorway and motioning Kate and Reed inside.

"Don't worry about the time," she said, throwing Jackson a warning look. "I'm sure you're hungry after your long drive."

"It's too late for dinner," Jackson said. "It's already cold."

"Cold cereal is supposed to be cold," Shelby said.

Jackson leaned against the wall as Reed and Kate entered. Reed thought he was just feigning anger, but there was real annoyance in his features. Then Reed caught sight of the table. Waffles and pancakes were stacked onto the plates, while a dozen boxes of cereal were lined up on the counter. Bacon, eggs, and other breakfast foods were also present, including sliced fruit, milk, and juice.

"Jackson," Kate groaned, also noticing the table. "I'm really sorry. I didn't realize you planned so much."

"It's not your fault," Jackson said, picking at his nails. "Ever since Reed started dating Kate, he hasn't been around much."

"Is that what this is about?" Shelby asked, looking between Jackson and Reed. "You miss your friend?"

"I didn't say that," Jackson sniffed.

"I'm sorry," Kate said. "I didn't know—"

"Don't," Shelby said. She reached out of view and appeared with her purse in hand. "Let's just leave them to hang out for a bit."

Kate looked between Shelby and Reed and smiled. "I think we can do that."

"What are we supposed to do?" Jackson protested.

"Play some video games or something," Shelby said, and leaned in to kiss him on the cheek.

"Video games aren't going to . . ."

But Shelby was already gone. With a huff, Jackson disappeared into the living room, leaving Reed with Kate at the door. Torn between staying with Kate and following Jackson, Reed shook his head.

"I'm guessing this isn't the ending you planned."

"I already got my date," she said. "I'll kiss you goodnight and you can hang out with your friend."

"You sure?" he asked.

She kissed him soundly and then smiled. "I can give you up for one night. You already fell for me."

She laughed and walked away, joining Shelby where she stood leaning against her car. Reed watched her go and then stepped into the living room. Jackson sat on the couch, picking at his fingernails.

"You shouldn't blame Kate," Reed said. "It's my fault I haven't been here much."

"Sure."

"I'm sorry."

"Fine."

Reed spotted the cereals on the counter and realized three were his favorites. Jackson was notorious for having cold cereal for dinner, and he'd likely planned the breakfast-for-dinner with that in mind.

"You got my favorites," Reed said, pointing to the three boxes.

"They're my favorites too."

Reed sighed and stepped to the TV. Turning on the Xbox, he picked up two controllers and sat down. Halo was an older game but one of their favorites. He didn't say anything, but he put the second controller next to him on the couch. Then he began to play alone.

The minutes ticked by as Reed played, the room filled with the sounds of dying aliens and grenades. Then Jackson released an explosive breath and picked up the second controller. Neither spoke, the silence stretching until Reed failed to see an enemy coming from behind.

"Watch your back," Jackson said.

"That's what I have you for," Reed said.

"Yeah, well, I can't do that if you're never here."

"I've never had a girlfriend before," Reed said. "It's new."

"Doesn't mean you have to forget your wingman."

"I didn't forget."

"If your wingman drives you to Florida and back, and then you disappear for two weeks, you did forget him."

Reed threw a grenade into a mix rushing Jackson. "Is that what this is about?"

Jackson grunted in annoyance. "You're like a brother, you know that? And not a little one, either, but a big one that gives me advice and helps me figure out what to do—like how I'm *supposed* to propose to Shelby."

"I have kind of been absent the last couple of weeks," Reed said with a grimace. "You never warned me that the first few days of a relationship can be so intense."

"My bad."

Reed laughed and recalled the events of the last two months. He'd become so preoccupied with Kate that he hadn't really thought about the impact on Jackson. Now he realized just how much he'd neglected their friendship.

"I am getting hungry," Reed said. "Care for a bowl of cereal?"

"Was that so hard to ask?"

Reed grinned and paused the game, and the two moved to the table. Reed heated a pair of waffles in the microwave and then sat down with a bowl of Golden Grahams. The tension evaporated as Reed asked about Shelby and how things were going.

Filling his mouth with a spoonful of Marshmallow Mateys, Jackson shook his head. "I think she knows I'm hiding something, and she almost found the ring."

"Where did you hide it?"

"In a box of cereal."

Reed burst into a laugh. "Which one?"

"Grape Nuts," Jackson said. "I never thought she would go for them, but she decided to try them yesterday."

"Do you know how you want to propose?" Reed asked.

As they discussed options Reed realized Jackson had bought the ring weeks ago, and had been waiting on Reed to help him plan the proposal. Resolving never to abandon his friend again, Reed dived into the discussion, intent on making up for his absence.

Chapter 6

Reed and Jackson talked until after midnight. Most of the time they talked about Jackson and Shelby, and ideas on how to propose. For the usually confident Jackson, proposing made him surprisingly nervous, which explained his frustration when Reed had abandoned him for Kate. After dinner they returned to the game and continued to talk while they played, but when Jackson went to the bathroom Reed pulled out his phone.

Everything okay? Kate had texted.

We're good, Reed responded. **I've just been very distracted lately.**

And I'm the distraction?

A really pretty one.

I've never seen Jackson upset, she said. **I feel bad.**

Don't, Reed said. **I just need to spend time with him. He has some things going on that he needs help with.**

With Shelby?

Reed wanted to explain but hesitated. It was Jackson's secret, after all. The sink in the bathroom came on and he didn't want Jackson to feel like he was still distracted. He didn't have time for a lengthy text but he didn't want to mislead either.

I have to go, he said. **Can I tell you later?**

Tomorrow for breakfast? she asked, and added a smiley face.

Lunch, he said. **I should probably hang out here in the morning.**

I'll pick you up.

See you then. I'll text you before I go to bed.

Jackson returned and Reed tucked his phone back into his pocket. Jackson glanced his way and shook his head. "How's Kate?"

"She feels bad."

Jackson abruptly released a self-deprecating laugh. "I can't really blame either of you. We spent months getting you and Kate together, and I knew how much you liked each other. I shouldn't be surprised at what you've become."

"So you're taking credit for us being together?"

"*I* was the one that helped Kate challenge you on your second date—*and* I kidnapped you and took you to Florida so you could get over Aura." His usual smile appeared. "You know I deserve credit."

"Really?"

"Really."

In the game, Reed turned and threw a grenade at Jackson. He dodged but threw one back, and for several furious seconds they battled, ignoring the alien threats until Jackson managed to kill Reed. As he waited to respawn, Reed leaned over and pushed Jackson.

"You don't get credit," he said. "But I couldn't have done it without you."

Jackson laughed, the lingering tension melting away. They continued to play but the conversation shifted to the upcoming semester, which would start on Monday. Jackson had three classes while Reed had two, and the finishing of his Thesis.

"I forgot about that," Jackson said. "You graduate in December, don't you?"

"It looks like it," Reed said, sprinting away from a new horde of digital enemies.

"So, don't you have that job waiting for you in New York?"

"Yeah," Reed said. "Dr. Caldin has a friend who joined a prestigious institute there. He's the one that recommended me for the internship."

"In December . . ." Jackson said.

"What are you getting at?" Reed asked, sparing him a glance.

"What are you going to do with Kate when you leave?"

Reed's surprise got him killed as a sniper picked him off. He hardly noticed. In the flurry of events with Kate he'd all but forgotten how soon he was going to be finished in Boulder. Four months and he would be gone.

But Kate would be staying.

Reed's graduation had been approaching for years, and in the last two weeks with Kate he hadn't thought at all about how this would affect the direction of their relationship. Now that he did, he recognized the impending collision.

He tried to shrug it off with a smile. "I've got four months to figure it out."

"Maybe," Jackson said. "But it'll come faster than you think."

Reed didn't respond, his shoulders dipping as if a tangible weight had settled on his back. It wasn't much, but he sensed that each passing week would increase the burden until time forced a decision.

"I still have time," he said, but a sliver of doubt threaded into his voice.

Jackson didn't press the issue and they continued to talk about Shelby. They played deep into the night and then Reed got ready for

41

bed. He texted Kate several times but didn't mention his concerns, telling himself he had plenty of time to figure out what he would do.

He fell asleep thinking about the internship. Dr. Caldin had made it clear it was a prestigious internship, one that paid well enough to live in New York City. More importantly, the other psychiatrists at the practice had connections into every doctoral program in the country, making it a perfect stepping stone into his career. But there were only a few slots a year, and Reed had banked everything on the opportunity, so he hadn't made any backup plans.

His forehead creased as he recalled the pre-graduate luncheon with other students. He'd talked to several representatives from other internships, several of which were nearly equal to his choice in New York. But is that what he wanted? Giving up New York would be hard, but if he could find an option that allowed him to continue his career and be with Kate . . .?

Ultimately he decided that he'd explore other possibilities. He was confident he could find another option as good as New York. Dr. Caldin would certainly help him, and he had other professors that might be able to help. He wanted to stay with Kate, and didn't want to choose between his career and his girlfriend. His decision made, the weight on his shoulders faded, allowing him to fall asleep.

But a sliver of doubt remained.

Volume 15: The Crazy Date

Chapter 1

As Kate got ready for the day, she texted Reed. The practice had become a habit and she relished the addition of him in her morning ritual. She messaged him throughout getting dressed and gathering her books. Classes had started the previous week and she collected her first homework of the semester, adding them to the bag before glancing to the calendar. In the last six months she'd marked every date with Reed, and the next was coming, soon. But he had yet to extend an invitation.

She shouldered her bag and then paused to pick up a picture of her with Reed, a soft smile lighting her face. The picture was from the Island Date, their fifth, and her favorite. Although they now spent a great deal of time together, she lived for the challenge dates.

She stepped into the living room to find two of her roommates lounging on the couches, both on their phones, the remains of a bowl of fruit on the coffee table. Kate sat down and picked up a strawberry.

"Good morning!" she said brightly, popping it into her mouth.

"You're smiling again," Ember said.

"Why does her happiness annoy you?" Brittney asked. "We *were* trying to get them together, remember?"

"It's been a month," Ember said. "They should have cooled off by now."

"You're the only person I know that could be angry with a puppy," Brittney said, exasperated.

Ember laughed at the reference to her temper, which now bordered on legendary. Two days ago she'd gotten a speeding ticket, and the officer probably still had burns on his face from Ember's meltdown. At just over five feet she was the shortest of the group. Her red hair matched her personality, but hid her fire beneath waves of beauty.

Brittney was the opposite. The girl was cute and generous, aspects usually overlooked when guys saw her weight. But in cooking she had no peer, especially when it came to her cookies. If they were any more addictive Kate would have to go into sugar rehab. Brittney was also the youngest of the roommates, and had just started her sophomore year.

Another bedroom door opened and Marta came down the stairs. Yawning, she caught sight of the three of them and sank onto the couch. She picked up a fork and stabbed at the cantaloupe, oblivious to the looks from the other three.

Of Puerto Rican descent, Marta retained the toned skin and dark eyes of her family. But she'd spent her whole life in the United States and spoke English better than Spanish. She was undeniably pretty, but her parents were adamant that she date only guys from Puerto Rico, a boundary that had loosened of late, partly because of Reed's and Kate's influence.

"What?" Marta asked, realizing they were staring.

Kate smiled and gestured to Ember. "She's annoyed at me for smiling too much."

"What do you expect?" Marta asked. "The girl's practically in love."

"I wouldn't go that far," Kate protested, but her smile widened.

Ember stabbed a finger at her. "Why do you get all the romance?"

"Because you helped orchestrate it," Kate said.

"She's got you there," Brittney said with a laugh.

"I love you girls, you know that?" Kate asked. She put an arm around Ember's shoulders and hugged her.

"Don't you have a class to get to?" Ember stabbing a strawberry like it was a foe to be vanquished.

"My mechanics lab," she said, glancing at the clock. "I need to go."

Brittney gestured to the table of fruit and toast. "Breakfast?"

Kate picked up a piece of toast and then strode to her backpack next to the door. "I lost track of time talking to Reed so I'm running late. Thanks for the toast."

"Have fun at class!" Brittney said.

Kate came to a halt in the doorway and looked back at her roommates suspiciously. "Is there a surprise waiting for me?"

"How would we know?" Ember said, shooting Brittney a sharp look.

Kate eyed her roommates as they shifted and avoided eye contact. Brittney in particular seemed engrossed in her phone, but her hand was fidgeting. She glanced up and grimaced when their eyes met, and Kate smirked.

"I'll call you after I find it," she said.

"Seriously, Brittney?" Ember demanded. "We almost had her."

Brittney raised her hands defensively. "Hey, with them dating it's getting a lot harder to surprise them . . ."

Kate shut the door and walked to her car, pleased that she'd managed to discover the plot. As she unlocked the door she pulled out her phone and called Reed. She didn't want to spoil the surprise, but that didn't mean she couldn't tease him a bit.

"Hey," he said, picking up on the first ring. "I'm about to step into class but I have a minute."

"I'm excited for class today," she said.

"Oh?"

"I think it's going to be *especially* interesting."

He groaned. "When did you figure it out?"

"Just a minute ago," Kate admitted, starting her car. "My roommates were a bit too excited for me to go to class."

"Don't forget I figured out the invitation for the Falling Date," he said. "So I guess we're even."

"I'll just have to be more clever next time," she said.

"I look forward to it." There was a door swinging open and then shutting. "Enjoy the invite."

"I'm sure I will. Meet after class for lunch?"

"Always."

She said goodbye and then drove to campus. She kept her eyes peeled. With Reed, the invite could be anywhere, in the parking garage, in a sign along the road. But there was nothing, and her anticipation mounted the closer she came to class.

Arriving at the engineering building, she made her way to the third floor lab and peeked through the window, but everything appeared normal. The classroom was almost full and Dr. Freeman was writing on the board.

She frowned, wondering if she'd somehow missed Reed's invitation. He had been spending a lot of time with Jackson. Had he been setting up something special? Then she entered the classroom and took a seat at one of the eight tables. Like all the mechanical labs, the room was filled with cabinets containing parts and electrical equipment. Buttons, switches, and tubing would be used throughout the semester for a variety of projects.

She greeted her group as she sat down. "Kent, Mike," she said, "how was your weekend?"

"Busy," they said in unison. "We had a big project to finish."

"But it's the second week of classes," she said with a frown, pausing in retrieving her notebook and pen. "What did you have to finish?"

They exchanged a look but were saved from answering when Dr. Freeman called the class to attention. "Before we begin today, a group would like to present an extra credit assignment to the class. Will those who participated please come forward?"

Kate turned to Kent and Mike, and asked. "What assignment . . .?"

But they were standing and walking to the front—as was every other student in the room. Confused, Kate stared as her entire class walked to the front, leaving her the only person remaining in her seat.

"We'll need a volunteer from the class," Mike said, smirking like Kate wasn't the only one still in her seat.

"What's going on?" Kate asked, rising to her feet.

She suddenly noticed all the smiles and realized exactly what was happening. Reed had gotten to her classmates. She looked to Dr. Freeman, who stood with his arms folded, a smile of satisfaction on his face.

"Don't look at me," he said. "Your boyfriend can be quite persuasive. I just agreed to give extra credit to those who participated."

"Participated in what?" she asked cautiously.

"Come and find out," Kent said.

He pointed to the front of the room, where a short hallway connected to a second lab. On this floor all the lab rooms were interconnected with back hallways, allowing students to access the equipment specific to each room.

"He recruited *all* of you?" she asked.

"We did it for the extra credit," a girl said, but the girl next to her elbowed her.

"The points were just bonus," she said.

Kate stepped to the doorway and looked around the frame. She glanced back uncertainly but the class stood silent, their expressions excited and impatient. Confused, Kate turned back and then noticed a stretch of tubing fastened to the other side of the door. Supported by tape, it curved into the adjoining room and out of sight. Balanced on the end was a marble, poised so, when touched, it would roll down the tubing like a cart on a roller coaster.

"Well?" Kent demanded. "Are you going to push it or not?"

"What does it do?" she asked, taking a step toward the other room.

"Don't!" several cried, and Mike shook his head.

"Follow the track and you'll find out."

Unable to keep the smile from her face, Kate reached toward the marble. Her fingertip brushed the glass and it began to roll down the tubing. Slow at first, it quickly accelerated as it approached the curve and banked into the dark room, where it landed in a motorized wheel that carried it upward and deposited it onto a second track. As it curved into the dark room Kate followed it and squinted into the gloom, watching the marble roll along a track about shoulder height.

It struck a second, larger marble which dropped off its ledge and landed in a basket attached to a pulley and the light switch. The weight caused the light to flip on, and Kate gasped as she saw what lay in the room.

Chapter 2

The room was *filled* with contraptions. Built of metal framework, engine parts, children's toys, and an assortment of household objects—she even spotted a plunger—they were placed about the room, and the marble was headed for the first.

She glanced at the class which had filed in behind her but their expressions were equally as excited. Then she looked back to the contraption just as the marble fell into a bucket. It descended to the floor, pulling a string attached to a balloon. As the balloon straightened, it dropped a trio of Mentos into a bottle of coke, which caused the soda to swell and lift a lever, dropping a matchbox car down another track. It tumbled into an accelerator belt that shot it across the room, where it triggered the unrolling of a sign on the wall.

Kate,

The marble reached the second contraption, setting off a series of toys that released the energy in the downed plunger. It sent another car to the wall of words, unrolling a second poster and a second word.

You've

The marble struck another a second marble, this one green, and the two balls activated two machines, one mechanical, one electrical. Wheels turned and light burst onto solar panels, sending two more cars into the wall, adding more words to the growing message.

Kate followed the marble, overwhelmed by how much effort her classmates had put into the machine. Most of them had been in her classes for the last two years, and her friends jumped about, proudly announcing what they had built.

It quickly became apparent that Reed had allowed each of her classmates to build a single machine, giving them the freedom to tailor the workings to their individual designs. Each was unique, some more electrical, while others used chemical or mechanical means to send a car to the wall.

"That was mine," Mike said, pointing to the one with the plunger.

"I'm next," a girl said, pointing to a machine built entirely of toys. "My nephews contributed the Legos," she added.

Kate praised all the contraptions as she followed the marble, working her way around the room while frequently looking to the sign unfolding over the chalkboard. In neat lettering it read:

Kate,

You're invited to a night of themes,

Where every game is not as it seems.

The words came to a stop there as the last contraption unfolded the final word. Then she realized the marble was still going. It disappeared down a track headed to the next room, drawing her gaze to Dr. Freeman.

"No," she breathed.

Dr. Freeman's smile was wry. "It's possible I liked the idea of some hands-on application and invited my fellow professors to participate."

Kate all but skipped after the marble, reaching the second room as the light clicked on. An entire other class and new machines greeted her, and the students shouted *"Surprise!"* like it was her birthday.

"I can't believe you did all this," she said, watching a new machine send another matchbox car into a new wall of signs.

"You've tutored half of us," Kent said. "And besides, the professors all agreed to give extra credit."

"Some less than others," Mike said, lowering his voice and glancing to the notoriously strict Dr. Hyde.

Stunned and overwhelmed, Kate followed the marble as it navigated machine after wondrous machine. Students laughed and pointed as the more inventive contraptions worked their magic, one sending a dart into a target across the room.

Our night of curiosity begins

At the store in unusual bins.

They continued to the next room, the contraptions going faster now, several triggering at once, moving so quickly it was impossible to watch them all. She protested but Kent was at her side, his phone out as he recorded the entire invitation. Others did the same, crying out as a particularly clever machine triggered a sign.

Then we play pool but not in a hall,

For the ground is where we'll hit the ball.

By the fourth classroom she could not speak. Hundreds of students milled about, their conversation revealing they had not seen the entire invitation unfolding. Many ducked into the preceding rooms and returned laughing and excited.

Last we savor a frozen treat

And 31 flavors we shall meet.

The marble continued down the last hall, speeding up as it went into a pipe that curved around a stairwell. Shouts of delight echoed up the brick walls as all the participants hurried after Kate, who arrived at the base of the stairs and followed the marble to the exterior door.

On the lawn outside the building, she found a collection of a dozen students standing around a catapult, which the marble triggered by rolling onto a button. The catapult fired, sending streams of shredded paper into the air while also pulling a chord. The rope went through a series of pulleys tied to trees and unfolded a banner from the neighboring building. The streams of paper struck the banner and fell to the ground in a curtain of shimmering fragments, framing the final message.

Please accept my invitation

For a night of intrigue and machination

Friday, 5:30

The crowd began to applaud and shout, voicing their appreciation of the machine. Kate turned to find hundreds of students gathered for the final presentation and tears welled in her eyes. She knew many of the students, although not all, and their expressions revealed that most had done it for more than points in a class.

"I can't believe you did all this," she said, fighting to speak.

"Believe it," Reed said, stepping into view.

"You're here?" she asked.

"You think I'd miss it?" he asked. "I slipped into your classroom when you went into the first room."

She swept her hand to the engineering department. "I don't think this is very fair. The competition is between you and I."

"What do you think?" Reed called, raising his voice. "You think I win this round?"

They shouted and applauded, and Kate grinned and shook her head. "You said you had class."

"I didn't say it was mine," he said.

He closed the gap and gathered Kate into his arms. "What do you say. Will you be my date?"

"All this for just a date?" a kid called. "You're not proposing?"

"Dude," his friend said. "It's a dating challenge. Don't you pay attention to anything?"

Kate hardly heard them, her attention locked solidly on Reed as they kissed. Students cheered anew, the sound washing over her in a wave of euphoria. When they parted he bore a smirk on his face.

"This doesn't mean you've won," she said.

"Only this round," he said smugly.

She couldn't argue with that. Even as the students set to cleaning up, Reed stayed until he had a real class to attend. Promising to return afterwards, he hurried away. Dr. Freeman took his place and helped her dismantle a machine of electrical wires, wood, and tape.

"He has a way of inspiring others," he said. "And a gift for leadership."

"I know," she said.

"Just make sure you keep him after he graduates."

"What do you mean?" she asked, turning to face him.

"He's in his last semester," Dr. Freeman said. "I understand he's accepted an offer for an internship in New York. I'm sorry, I thought you knew."

She recalled Reed had mentioned the internship several months ago, and tried to brush it off. "I did, I just forgot."

Dr. Freeman inclined his head, his expression revealing he was not entirely convinced. "Good luck to you both," he said, and then strode away.

Kate shook her head, confused by the exchange. Had he kept it from her? Or just forgotten to talk about it? Her frown deepened as she worked to disassemble the machine, but forced her doubt aside when more of her classmates approached.

Reed returned an hour later and she buried her doubt. He seemed lighthearted and excited, and endured the endless congratulations with a touch of humility that she'd come to admire. If there was any doubt about their future it did not show on his face, and she resolved to wait until he brought it up.

He remained at her side as they helped with the cleanup. Some of the professors cancelled class and had their engineering students help, while others, such as Dr. Hyde, insisted their students attend. Regardless, the machines were all taken down in short order and they were finally alone on their way to a late lunch.

"Everything okay?" he asked.

"Fine," she said, flashing a smile.

"Are you sure?" he asked. "You've been rather quiet. Was the invite too much?"

"No," she said hastily. "It was stunning. I just have a lot on my mind."

His gaze lingered on her and she did her best to keep her thoughts from her face. They had hardly been dating a month and she had no right to tell him what to do after graduation. What if he chose New York? What did that mean for them? She couldn't leave her program and it was too late to apply to schools in New York. Was she willing to go for him? Was he willing to stay?

The questions bombarded her but she forced a smile. "Ready to eat?" she asked, and hoped he would bring it up before she exploded.

Chapter 3

She managed to keep her doubt contained until Friday, but mostly because Reed said he had homework. He was also working on his thesis, which he would have to present to a committee soon.

The blondes sensed her turmoil and tried to get her to talk, but this time she resisted. The days sped by and Friday came, with Reed arriving promptly at 5:30. He smiled and walked her to his ancient Camry that had already quit once on a date.

"Hungry?" he asked.

"Starving," she said.

He handed her a piece of paper with the words of his invite. "Did you figure out the clues?"

She shook her head. "I tried, but I think I only got the last line. Thirty-one flavors has to be Baskin Robbins."

"It is," he said, raising his eyebrow. "Is that all?"

Despite her doubts, his smile was contagious. "What are we doing that's tinted?"

"Dinner first," he replied, pulling into the parking lot of a grocery store. As they walked in he explained, "We are going to split up and take four aisles each." He handed her ten dollars. "You have drinks and dessert. I have main course and appetizer."

"What are you getting?"

"That's the twist," he said. "We won't know the other half of dinner until we meet back up."

"So I have no idea what you're getting?"

"Nope," he said. "I got the idea from your dessert on our second date. I figured we could try it at dinner."

"So now you're learning from me?" she asked, raising an eyebrow.

"A great deal," he said, coming to a halt and brushing her hair behind her ear. "Ready?"

"Are you going to give me a hint what you're getting?" she asked.

"Nope," he replied, and then asked for her phone. "One more thing," he said, setting a timer. "We're on the clock. Five minutes is all you get."

"To pick both?"

"Yep," he said, his eyes lighting with anticipation. "It's a race."

She grinned. "On your mark."

"Get set," he said.

"Go!" they said in unison and raced toward their respective aisles.

She hurried down the ice-cream aisle, hunting for something that sounded good. Spotting a razzleberry pie, she snagged it and then made her way to the drink aisle. Feeling the weight of time, she darted back and forth, trying to guess what he would choose.

She could pick a regular soda and play it safe, or go for an unusual soda like Jones. Or she could choose something more exotic. Among the juices she spotted a Mexican fruit juice and smiled, but just as she reached for it she was assailed by doubt. The doubt was unusual— especially with Reed, but it found a foothold. Bound by hesitation, she paced back and forth until opting for a root beer.

She regretted the choice all the way to the register, wondering about the source of the doubt. Since the Lantern Date, she'd never worried so much about their relationship. Did it have to do with his upcoming graduation? Or was it a chink in their relationship? Spotting Reed, she joined him and he held up his sack.

"I've got Stove Top Stuffing for dinner and strawberries for the appetizer. What do you have?"

"Pie and root beer," she replied.

"Great," he said. "We'll go back and while it cooks we'll start the game, the List."

"I think you mentioned that before," she said.

"It's one of my favorites," he said.

They returned to the car and drove back to his apartment. Although they smiled and talked, he kept glancing her way as if trying to crack a difficult puzzle. She avoided talking of school, afraid that it would reveal her doubts.

"Jackson and Shelby are playing basketball with a group of friends," Reed said, shouldering his way into the kitchen. "You ready to cook dinner together?"

"I'll start with the strawberries," she said. "I've never cooked stuffing, but my mom always made it on Thanksgiving."

"I'm sure we can figure it out," Reed said, examining the box.

They set about cooking their surprising meal, and Kate all but forgot her fears regarding Reed's graduation. They brushed each other against the stove and sink, their arms touching, their eyes catching each other as they talked.

She thought several times of their last challenge date, of them kissing under the waterfall. With any other guy, they would have had sex then and there, but Reed had irritatingly managed to keep his boundaries. Still, she wondered if there were cracks in his resolve.

Although they'd had many dates, this night was oddly the most intimate. They talked and laughed like a married couple, their

59

conversation easy as they worked next to each other to prepare the meal. Kate imagined what it would be like to be with Reed in such a setting, and for the first time in her life, imagined what it would be like to be a wife.

Would it be cooking dinner together? Smiles and kisses shared next to the stove? Or would it be fights in the hall and slammed doors? Cold nights spent alone, wondering when an angry husband would return? She glanced at Reed as he unwrapped the pie and placed it on a pan in the oven, and dared to hope of a life together.

"Are the strawberries ready?"

"Almost," she said.

Reed seemed to sense the intimacy of the night, but rather than shrink from it, he cast her amused looks and placed his hand on her back as he passed, their eyes connecting briefly while he stirred the pot.

"Ow!" she cried.

Her focus on Reed, the knife had slipped and sliced into her finger. She winced as blood welled up and dripped into the sink. She dropped the strawberry and caught a paper towel as Reed appeared at her shoulder.

"Are you okay?"

"Just cut myself," she said, pulling back the paper towel to examine the injury, but blood welled into view.

"Looks deep," he said.

"You're too distracting," she said, wincing again. "You're very attractive when you cook."

"You should see me vacuum," he said, his lips twitching. "In the meantime, can I get you a Band-Aid?"

"Please," she said.

He disappeared and she used his absence to regain control of herself. She'd enjoyed the image of a life with Reed but did her best to quash the hope. Although they'd been dating for seven months, they'd only been together for one, and she couldn't let herself fall so far that she lost touch with reality.

He returned and wrapped the bandage around her finger. She swallowed, annoyed that he had such an effect on her. She was the one with more dating experience, so why was she trembling? His touch made her shiver, and then he kissed her finger.

"Sorry," he said, his smile all but melting her into the floor.

"Nothing to apologize for," she said.

"You have the same effect on me, you know," he said.

"I'm not sure I do," she said.

"Trust me," he said. "You do."

Held fast by the intensity of his gaze, she caught a glimpse of just how much he desired. He held himself in check, but a part of him wanted to let go. They were standing close, her hand still in his, the proximity so close she could feel his leg against hers, his other arm around her back, but he did not pull her close.

She swallowed. "Are you saying you want to . . ."

"I do," he said quietly. "But you mean enough to me that I want to wait."

"Most guys say the opposite," she said, touching his cheek.

"I don't want to be most guys," he replied. "Especially with you."

The timer went off and they both jumped. They laughed in unison and he stepped to the stove, pulling the pot off the burner. The moment had lapsed and she expected to be disappointed. Instead she felt safe. Whatever happened, she would never have to worry about Reed pushing boundaries. Not because he didn't want to, but because he cared about her enough to hold himself in check.

Chapter 4

"Ready for the List?" he asked, scooping their stuffing onto plates.

She poured the strawberries into two bowls and set them on the table, taking a seat next to Reed. "Ready," she said, taking a bite.

"Mountains or beach?" he asked.

She raised an eyebrow. "That's a rather basic question, isn't it?"

He pretended to be offended. "Don't disparage the List. You might say beach and tell me it's because you love the sand in your toes, or that you like to surf, both things I wouldn't know about you. Or you might say mountains because you enjoy the snow."

"What would you say?" he asked.

"Mountains," he said. "I love the snow and winter, and love to snowboard."

"I remember you mentioned that," she said. "I've never been."

"Then I get the extreme privilege of teaching you," he said with a smile. "Now your turn."

Torn, she took a strawberry and considered her answer. "You know I love hiking and the mountains," she said. "But I would have to say the beach. There's just something magical about the ocean at twilight."

"The sun setting over the ocean is nice," he agreed.

"Next question?"

"Stars or storms?" he asked.

Surprised by the clever question, she considered her answer. "Storms," she said. "Wrapped in a blanket while a storm rages is indescribable."

"Me too," he said. "Especially a snowstorm. Reading when the snow is falling, all sound muffled and quiet, was one of my favorite things growing up."

"I thought you grew up in Tallahassee."

"My family moved there when I was kid," he said.

"I didn't know that," she said, skewering her last strawberry. "Where did you live before that?"

"Colorado," he said. "Denver, actually."

"You lived here?" she asked, surprised.

"I don't remember much," he said. "But I remember learning to snowboard and playing in the snow."

As they ate, the questions continued. Batman or Superman. Winter or summer. Raspberry or strawberry. Each resulted in stories and laughter, of events and moments from their lives. They only made it through six questions by the time they were done with dinner and dessert, and she'd learned more about him than she'd ever expected.

They both liked raspberries, him because his grandfather had raspberry bushes in his garden, her because of raspberry pie her mother had made every holiday. She preferred summer while he liked winter. Both liked Batman.

"We'd better go," he said, checking the clock on the stove. "We have the activity to get to."

"It's after eight," she said, surprised.

The remains of their odd meal lay scattered across the table and she tried to recall when she'd finished her pie. It had been delicious, but the conversation with Reed dominated her attention.

64

"This activity is better at night," he said, rising and gathering his keys from the counter.

She recalled the invitation. "We play pool but not in a hall, for the ground is where we'll hunt the ball. What's that supposed to mean?"

"You'll see," he said, his eyes sparkling with mischief.

They cleaned up their dinner and returned to his car, but he stopped on the way out and picked up a pair of pool cues from the coat closet, which didn't have any coats. She raised an eyebrow at the choice.

"Most pool tables come with their own cues," she said. "But I suppose we aren't playing in a hall?"

"Nope," he said. "I hope you don't mind getting a little dirty."

She looked down at her jeans and dark shirt. "Are we getting dirty together?"

"Probably," he said with a laugh.

They returned to his car and drove to the southern side of town. The List continued in the car, but they only got through a single question, the stories inspired by the question taking the entire drive to tell, and only stopped when they pulled into a mini-golf course.

"I thought we were playing pool," she said.

"We are," he replied. "But as you'll recall, I did say it would be on the ground."

She frowned, and then realized what he was suggesting. "We're going to play miniature golf . . . with pool cues?"

"Yes," he said.

She laughed, the sound tinged with admiration. "Really?"

"I brought towels if you don't want to lay on the ground."

"I don't mind," she said, excited at the prospect.

They walked up to the hut at the entrance, their pool cues in hand. The girl behind the counter saw them and smiled, rising to her feet. Then her eyes flicked to the pool cues and her eyes widened. She turned to Reed like he was someone to be worshiped.

"Reed?" she asked. "I wasn't sure you'd follow through."

"Thanks for letting us do this," Reed said.

"Are you kidding?" the girl asked, her tag identifying her as Anna. "This is the most exciting thing I've ever seen on this job."

Reed paid and they made their way to the first hole, a windmill that spun over the track. The night traffic was light, with only a few other visitors to the course, another couple and a trio of girls on the seventeenth hole.

He placed the ball on the mat and then eyed the track like a pool player examining the angles. Kate stifled a laugh at his serious expression. Then Reed turned to Kate, a grin on his face as he offered the stick to her.

"Would you like to go first?"

"Such a gentleman," she said, taking the stick. "Or is it because you've never done this and want me to go first?"

"Can't it be both?"

She laughed and laid down on the ground, lining up the cue for a shot. She was highly aware of Reed watching her back and tried not to let it distract her as she aimed. A smile on her face, she timed her shot to miss the windmill and then hit the ball.

The impact sent the ball tumbling away. Her aim was good but she hadn't hit the ball hard enough and it slowed as it approached the windmill. She cringed when it reached the top of the incline, the windmill spinning towards the golf ball. The windmill and ball came together, the ball bouncing off the wood and spinning under the structure.

She watched it shoot the gap and careen down the following slope to the circle of green. It missed the hole and bounced off the far wall, ricocheting back toward the hole. It slowed but continued to roll . . . and tipped in for a hole-in-one.

She rose to her feet and turned to Reed, who stood, dumbfounded. She leaned up to kiss him on the cheek. "That's how it's done," she said.

"I should have gone first," he said ruefully.

"No," she said. "I think I like going first."

He grinned and lay down, using his own stick to aim at the ball. She watched him, admiring the view as he sighted along the pool cue, wondering why she got to be so lucky to have him as her boyfriend.

He hit the ball and it went spinning away. It missed the windmill by inches and went straight down the slope, but bounced out of the hole and spun away. He scowled and rose to his feet, turning to her.

"Just missed the corner pocket," he said.

"You're good at pool," she said. "Where'd you learn?"

"My sister, actually," Reed said. "She coped with my parent's breakup by hanging out in our basement. She got so she could beat us all, but I did pick up a few things."

"You still missed," she said, poking him in the stomach. "And I'm winning."

"The night is young," he said.

They moved to the green and he crouched next to his ball. The bushes didn't allow for a full shot so he unscrewed the bottom half of the cue and used just the top half. Still, the gap forced him to contort his body in a laughable pose to hit the ball. She snorted in disbelief as he tapped the ball into the hole.

"Does mine do that?" She motioned to the detachable cue.

"Of course," he said. "You didn't think I'd give myself an advantage, did you? Besides, we both know you play. I asked your mom and she said you played with your brothers. That's why I thought you'd like this game."

"I still think it's strange that you've talked to my mom," she said.

"I've only spoken to her a few times," he said. "There were a few of our early dates that none of your roommates could help with, and Ember gave me her number. Do you mind?"

"No," Kate said. "But she would probably like to talk to you more."

"Why do you say that?"

"Because she's always wants to talk to the guys I date. She doesn't realize it's weird." She gestured to the tee of the second hole. "Your turn to go first."

He lay down and took aim, and the ball went sailing into a tube that connected to a second platform. She followed suit, but this time he lay down at her side. She glanced his way and raised an eyebrow, but he merely smiled.

"Are you trying to distract me?"

"Of course," he said, leaning over to brush his lips against her cheek. "You don't mind, do you?"

She smiled and shook her head. "It's not going to work."

She trembled when his breath brushed her neck, and struggled to focus, but failed utterly, the ball bouncing off the wall and missing the tube entirely. It fell down a slope to a different platform.

"Turnabout is fair play," she said, standing and facing him.

"I wouldn't have it any other way," he replied.

Chapter 5

Pool golf was surprisingly easier than using a club, except when the ball ended up close to a wall. In those settings they had to use the stick like a club, inevitably sending the ball in unexpected directions.

"Quadruple bogey," Reed said, filling in the scorecard.

"You don't have to sound so smug," Kate said sourly.

"Actually I do," Reed said. "Or have you forgotten when you tickled me at the pirate ship. I got a triple bogey."

She sniffed. "Not my fault you can't keep your emotions in check."

"Tickling is cheating," he said.

"No it's not," she said, laying down on the fifth hole.

"Fine," he said. "But that mean's it's fair game."

She realized her mistake and tried to backtrack but he was already at her side. She began to giggle as his fingers brushed her waist and fought to keep the cue lined up on the hole. She struggled to brush him off long enough to make the shot.

"You have only yourself to blame," he said.

"Stop!" she cried, laughing. "This is impossible. I agree, no tickling."

He retreated. "I don't recall that on the rules at the front of the course, but I'm sure it was implied."

She lined up her shot and hit the ball before he could do anything else, her haste sending the ball up the slope and into the wrong funnel. It tumbled down a hidden tube and popped into view on a different section, ricocheted off two walls before bouncing into a channel that led to the hole.

The competition heated up by the tenth hole, and by the fourteenth it was an inferno. Both teased and cajoled, making every effort to prevent the other from making a shot. They agreed to no touching, but that left a world of possibilities.

Kate considered flashing him, but decided that would push it too far. Instead, she offered a sexy pose and leaned against a lighthouse, running her hand down her hip. He shook his head and she noticed him swallowing like his mouth had gone dry.

"If I stay here," he called. "Will you stay there?"

She laughed and shifted, flipping her hair over her shoulder. "Nope. Three seconds and I walk away."

He hit the ball, but it went tumbling in the wrong direction. It bounced off two walls and ended up behind a barrier, even farther than its original location. Kate laughed and skipped to him, kissing him on the cheek as he stood.

"I think I'm winning."

"Oh?"

She grinned. "Distracting you is the best type of game."

They battled under a waterfall but took a brief break from the game to kiss in the tunnel, the setting a reminder of their last date. Then they continued to wage war on the course, each attempting to distract the other. As they neared the end of the course they checked the score and realized they were both doing equally badly.

"We'd probably be doing great if we weren't trying to sabotage each other," she said.

71

"What would be the fun in that?" he asked.

"No more distractions," she said. "I mean to win this game."

"Bring it on," he said.

The next two holes were all serious, or as serious as they were able to be. He kept a respectable distance, but his just standing in her peripheral vision was a distraction enough. The light shining on the volcano cast him in soft shadows, enhancing the muscular curve to his torso. Had he always been that tall?

She missed and muttered a curse as it failed to make the incline. She then vacated the spot so he could shoot. He missed as well, and she was gratified to know she was equally as distracting even when not trying to be. When they finished the seventeenth hole she stooped and picked up her ball.

"I'm beginning to realize what will happen if we are on opposite teams," she said.

"What's that?"

"We're both going to lose," she said as they walked to the final hole. "Just look at our score. Aside from the first couple of holes, we've done terribly."

"Depends on your perspective," he said.

"The score shows us both losing," she said, pointing to the paper in his hands.

"That's not what matters to me," he said, catching her about the waist and spinning her close.

"So the score doesn't matter?"

"I didn't come here to play golf," he said, "I came here to be with you."

She leaned up and kissed him soundly, her free hand wrapping around his neck to hold him tight. Then she pulled away with a giggle and whipped out the paper, scribbling in the scores of the latest hole.

"I caught up!" she cried.

He laughed and followed her to the last hole, where they decided to shoot at the same time. They lay down next to each other and settled in. As Kate lined up the shot she realized they were reclining just inches from each other. The course had emptied and the hole was behind the shack, out of view from anyone. She shifted and met his gaze, and he flashed his easy smile.

"I've always wanted to do this date," he said.

"You've planned it before?"

"Just never worked out," he replied. "I think I was meant to pool golf with you."

"I'm glad it was with me," she said. "But I still want to win."

He sighed and shook his head, but his eyes sparkled with amusement. "We'll see."

"And no throwing the game," Kate warned. "I hate that."

He grinned and settled in. "One hole. One victor. You ready?"

"Yes," she said.

She took aim and sighted for the hole beneath a water tower. The ball had to be precise, passing through several narrow bridges before dropping into the hole. If her aim was off, it could fall to either side and she'd have to go uphill.

"You first," she called.

"If you're sure," he said.

She heard the stick strike the ball, the sound indicating it had struck dead center. The ball hurtled to the first bridge, passing it in the center and easily passing the second. To Kate's dismay, it rolled straight into the hole, and the sound of the disappearing ball echoed back to her like a smug laugh.

"Your turn," he said.

"I *know*," she said.

With the pressure on, she gathered herself, lining up the shot so it could follow his ball for a hole-in-one. This was it, the chance to match his score, to prove he hadn't distracted her more than she had distracted him. She pulled her arm back and hit the ball, sending it speeding down the green—directly into the bridge wall.

With a clang of metal it rolled down the slope into a lower section of the green. Groaning, she rose to her feet and walked to her ball. Reed fell into step beside her and she glanced to see a smile on his face.

"It was a good game," he said.

"Don't patronize me," she said.

He laughed and waited for her to hit the ball a second time. Mercifully, she succeeded in hitting the ball into the final hole and watched the ball disappear from sight. Then she sighed and stood to face him.

"It was a close game, and although you cheated, you still won."

"Me?" he asked, his expression shocked. "Cheat? I would never."

She cocked her head to the side. "You know, I don't think you ever would."

He realized what she meant and raised an eyebrow. "I meant in the game."

"I know," she said, patting him on the chest.

They made their way to the car, passing the entrance hut on their way out. Several newcomers cast them strange looks, but Anne called out to them and waved.

"Please come again!" she called.

"I'm sure we will," Kate said. "I want a rematch."

"Did you see her watching us?" Reed asked as they walked to the car.

"She spied on us?" Kate asked.

"Can you blame her?" Reed said. "We played pool on her course. She was curious. I also saw her taking pictures."

Abruptly Anne appeared and rushed to them. "I'm sorry!" she said. "I didn't realize you were *the* Reed and Kate."

"You know us?" Kate asked.

"From Ember's blog," she said. "Can I get a picture with you? I love the dates you've gone on."

Kate exchanged a look with Reed and they agreed, and the girl whipped her phone out and took a selfie with them. Still gushing about their blog, she hurried back to the couple waiting at the course. When she was gone Kate leaned over to Reed.

"That was weird," she said.

"Our challenge is gaining attention," he said.

"Are you annoyed?" she asked.

"I was," he admitted. "But I'm glad others are liking how I date. Ready for dessert?"

She smiled. "To Baskin Robbins."

"How did you know?"

"31 flavors?" she asked. "What else could be?"

His smile was positively wicked. "You may know the place, but you don't know the dessert."

Chapter 6

"You want what?"

They were at Baskin Robbins, as Kate had guessed, but she could never have imagined his request. It was half an hour before closing time and no one was in the shop. The kid behind the counter, who couldn't have been more than seventeen, stared at Reed like he'd sprouted a second head.

"I'd like a sample amount of all the flavors on a single cone please."

"What's the matter?" another girl drifted over. "What does he want?"

Reed repeated the request and the girl smiled. "Tammy warned us you'd be coming in. Joey can make one while I make the other."

"You called ahead?" Kate murmured as the two employees set about making the strange ice cream cones.

"I didn't want them to refuse," he whispered back.

"But all 31 flavors?"

He grinned at her. "A night so tinted, remember? Can't just have a regular flavor."

Kate read them as the girl put a tiny amount of each flavor into the cup. Banana Nut Fudge, Chocolate Almond, and Cherry Macaroon were added to Eggnog, Lemon Crisp, and Raspberry Sherbet. The two employees were quickly swept up in the moment, laughing as they added strange flavors next to each other. When it was finally presented, the rainbow colored ice-cream cone was larger than Kate had expected, and she accepted it gingerly.

"I can't believe we're doing this," she said.

"*I* can't believe you're doing it," the girl said, ringing up the order.

"It's the Full Robbins," Reed said with a smile. "I've always wanted to try it."

Kate took an experimental lick and tasted several odd flavors. She grimaced and turned it over, trying again with better results. The employees watched her to see her response but ultimately she smiled.

"It's odd," Kate said. "But every bite is unique."

Reed accepted his own cone and took a bite, his expression twisting in surprise. Kate glanced back as they left, and saw Joey grab a cone and start making his own Full Robbins. Kate smiled and took another bite, blending Chocolate Mint with Peppermint Stick.

"Tonight really has been fun," she said as they walked to his car. "You've taken all the normal facets of a date and made them better. I don't think I'll ever look at ice cream the same way again."

"Sometimes the most fun dates are simple ones with a twist," he replied. He grimaced after a bite. "Eggnog and Coffee do not mix well."

They laughed and experimented with different flavors. All blended together it was hard to discern the flavors by the color, leading to surprising and sometimes delicious combinations. The tastes were fleeting and impossible to replicate in the same cone.

"Are you okay?" he asked.

"Of course," she said. "Why do you ask?"

"When I picked you up, you just seemed burdened."

She blinked in surprise, and realized she'd all but forgotten her concerns of the previous days. Time with Reed seemed to take fears and burdens and cast them aside, like he was an emotional epicenter that did not permit the presence of fear.

"I realized a few days ago that you graduate in December," she said.

"Ah." He said it like he'd expected the question.

"You mentioned it a few months ago, but that was before we got together," she said. "Then Dr. Freeman reminded me about your internship in New York."

"And you were worried."

"I was," she admitted, glancing his way to gauge his reaction. "Are you leaving after graduation?"

"I was going to," he said, pulling into her driveway and putting the car in park. "But now I find my excitement has waned."

All at once the words tumbled from her mouth. "We've only been dating for a month—I know that, and I know I don't have any right to ask you to stay. It's your career and you've been working toward these goals for years, but if you—"

His kiss silenced her, the passion driving her doubts into a corner, casting it aside as if it was nothing. She clung to him, her arm reaching around his neck and threading into his hair. When they parted he held her gaze, his blue eyes intense.

"You have nothing to worry about."

"But your internship. Dr. Freeman said it was a prestigious opportunity where they only choose a few candidates and they chose you and—"

He kissed her again, and again her worries faded, replaced by a burning in her gut that spread to her throat. This time when they parted she looked into his eyes and scowled.

"I don't like how easy it is for you to erase my worry."

"Yes, I was offered the position a couple of months ago. No, I'm not planning on leaving anymore, because I'm looking at other potential internships."

"Why would you not take it?" she asked, her eyes widening.

"Isn't it obvious?" he asked, and kissed her again.

"I told you that wasn't fair," she said, her breathing ragged.

"I like this new power," he said, a trace of smugness in his tone. "But you have wielded it on me, so you have no one to blame but yourself."

"You're really not going to go?"

"Not if I can help it," he said. "I'm scheduled to talk to Dr. Caldin next week. He said he'd reach out to a few friends and see what he could find."

A surge of elation burned away Kate's previous fear. They'd been sort of dating for seven months, and now Reed was placing her as his priority, even above his career. Even Jason had always chosen his career goals over hers. He may have invited her to be part of them, but they had always been his.

As they talked about his other possibilities her elation gradually faded into guilt. Was he sacrificing everything for her? Did their relationship merit such a choice? Would they still be together in December?

"I think you should go to New York," she blurted.

He paused. "Why?"

"I don't want you to give up something you'll regret," she said.

He laughed lightly and leaned in. "Right now, leaving would be my greatest regret."

"Are you sure?" she asked.

"I have other options," he said. "I'm late in applying but my grades are excellent and I have the highest recommendation by my professors. I'm confident I can find something closer."

Closer to you.

He didn't say it, but his fleeting smile implied it. Her guilt shrank before the affection in his eyes. "I don't want you to regret it," she said.

"Never," he replied.

They got out of the car and he walked her to her door. As his arms folded around her back she looked up into his eyes and smiled, suddenly intensely grateful for whatever God had blessed them to meet.

"I'm sorry we didn't finish the List," she said.

"I'm not worried," he said. "I look forward to playing with you in the future."

"And I want a rematch on pool golf," she said.

"Anytime," he said, and then amended. "Anytime except Friday. I have a quiz in Advanced Anatomy."

She went up on her toes and kissed him. Then she turned and opened her door but he caught her hand and held on. She cast a look back to find him smiling at her, his eyes sparkling with amusement.

"Sleep well, Kate. I look forward to your next invite."

"I'll see you tomorrow?" she asked.

"Let's do breakfast at my place," he said. "I'll make waffles."

"I'll see you then," she said.

She smiled and then slipped inside. When the door shut she leaned against it and closed her eyes, releasing a sigh. She imagined Reed walking to his car and driving away, but it seemed like he never left.

"You have it bad."

Kate opened her eyes to find Brittney sitting at the table. The clock on the wall marked the time as after one, late for a date with Reed, who preferred to finish by midnight. Ember and Marta were asleep on the couch, sprawled as if they'd been waiting for Kate's arrival.

Kate walked to the table and sank into a seat next to Brittney. "You think so?"

"It's obvious to everyone," Brittney said with a smile. She leaned back in her chair and cocked her head to the side. "I've never seen two people more perfect for each other."

"We've only been dating a month," Kate said.

"You've been dating for *seven* months," she said. "And you've acted like this from the beginning."

"What do you mean?" Kate asked.

"The way you look at him—and the way he looks at you—has been the same since the first night. It may have taken you a few months to get rid of your baggage, but what you feel hasn't changed."

"Is that what you see?" Kate asked.

"That's what we all see," Brittney said, sweeping a hand to their slumbering roommates. "It's why we help you plan the invites, because we see in you what we want for ourselves."

"I'm sorry," she said.

"For what?" Brittney said, rising to her feet. "You've made us believe in love again."

"I think it's a little early for that word," Kate said, trying to keep the flutter in her heart from showing on her face.

"Is it?" Brittney said. When Kate didn't respond Brittney smiled and nodded as if she understood. "Good night, Kate."

Unable to speak, Kate watched Brittney go to her room. She thought she knew how much she felt for Reed, but was her emotion deeper than she realized? Even as she lay in bed that night the question burned.

Was she in love with Reed?

Volume 16: The Bad Date

Chapter 1

Five minutes before the end of class, Reed slipped into the back of the room and took an empty seat. He'd taken the class in his sophomore year and it had been the first time he'd met Dr. Caldin. Now the professor was his graduate advisor.

Dr. Caldin glanced his way but continued his lecture. The classroom was large and nearly full, with over a hundred students taking the required class on Abnormal Psychology. Most were paying attention, while a few were attempting to be sly while texting on their phones.

Dr. Caldin never missed anything. Without pausing in his lecture, he scribbled a note on the book in front of him, no doubt marking the trespassers. Dr. Caldin had each student sign a paper on the first day committing to no cell phone use, and those who broke their agreement saw their grades gradually tumble.

Reed hid a smile. At first glance the man appeared dry and quiet, and many students assumed he was an easy grader. Those who did were severely disappointed when they discovered he'd recorded every infraction throughout the semester. If they complained he merely took out the contract they had signed and gave them a copy.

Students that heeded the warning at the start of the semester saw an entirely different side to the professor. Affable and amusing, he was a staunch supporter for the diligent, and he'd helped countless students get into doctoral programs across the country. His word carried a lot of weight from his time as a renowned psychologist. But this time, Dr. Caldin's comments shifted toward the end of his lecture.

"Abnormal behavior is frequently difficult to discern," Dr. Caldin said. "But one technique is to observe a shift from previously documented behavior. If you examine your previous dating life, you might see several moments of abnormal behavior. However, the most interesting elements are not the behavior, but the catalyst that causes the behavior." His eyes flicked to Reed and his lips twitched with amusement. "Always keep an eye on the catalyst."

Reed stifled a laugh as Dr. Caldin dismissed the class with a wave of his hand. Then the students filed out. Reed waited as the mass of students gathered their books and laptops and departed, and then made his way to the front of the classroom.

"Mr. Thompson," Dr. Caldin said, nodding.

"Thank you for making time to meet," Reed said. "I know how full your schedule is."

"It's not a problem," Dr. Caldin said. "But I must admit, I was surprised at your request."

They walked to Dr. Caldin's office and Reed took a seat in front of his desk. Unlike his classroom, which had posters of brain scans and interviews from famous studies, his office had pictures of movies from early cinema. Many of the black and white posters were of films written by Hitchcock.

"I've managed to compile a list of the remaining internships with slots opening in January," Dr. Caldin said.

He retrieved a paper from a drawer in his desk and passed it to Reed, who leaned back to read the list of his options. He frowned as he realized that the paper was mostly blank, with only two items on the top. One in Denver, one in Cheyenne.

"There aren't many that fit your parameters," Dr. Caldin said.

"I knew it was going to be difficult," Reed said. "I'm just glad there is something on this paper."

"The Cheyenne practice is run by Dr. Gladman," he said. "His practice is more pharmaceutical and deals with addiction recovery."

"And Denver?"

"Dr. Borges," he said. "They deal mostly with depression and anxiety disorders."

Reed tried to keep the disappointment from his face. He'd known his options would be limited this late, but hoped for something in marriage and family counseling. Both of the potential options lacked appeal, but in his current circumstances he didn't have much choice.

"There are a few other possibilities, but they are further out," Dr. Caldin said, as if reading his mind. "Unfortunately, the nearest possible internship that does marriage counseling is in Kansas City."

"Too far," Reed replied with a shake of his head. "I want to be within a few hours of Boulder."

"Are you certain?"

"I am."

"I thought you might say that," Dr. Caldin said. He sat back and peered over his glasses. "I've taken the liberty of reaching out to the directors of both local practices. Although it's past the deadline, they've agreed to receive your application on my recommendation."

"Thank you, professor. I really appreciate your support."

Dr. Caldin's expression remained sober. "I need to make it clear that, even with my letter of recommendation, your chances are slim. You are a gifted student and I'm confident you will be a great psychiatrist, but these practices are already well into the review process, with some applicants already chosen."

"I understand," Reed said. "I'll reach out and submit my applications within the next day or two."

"May I ask you a question?" he asked.

"Of course," Reed said.

"The internship in New York is one of the most prestigious in the country, and they only accept four students each year. From what Dr. Dickson has said, you are the best applicant they've seen in years. Are you sure you want to give it up for Kate?"

"What makes you think I'm doing this for her?"

Dr. Caldin raised an eyebrow. "I'm not blind. Kate has ignited a fire in you—and it's obvious to anyone you meet."

Reed shrugged but couldn't resist a return smile. "She has changed things a great deal."

Dr. Caldin gestured to the paper in Reed's hands. "Both of these internships are decent, but nowhere near the caliber of Dr. Dickson's office. Going to New York will open doors to every doctoral program in the country. It's obvious what you feel for Kate, but giving up on this will mean sacrificing your dream."

"Maybe I have a new dream," Reed said.

"Perhaps," Dr. Caldin said. "But is your commitment shared?"

Reed considered his response and his thoughts turned to their most recent date, when they'd been playing pool golf. He'd watched her face, the curve of her smile. He didn't know the depth of Kate's feelings, but he wanted to find out.

"Everything in life is a gamble," Reed said. "What matters is not the risk, it's the reward—and Kate is the reward I want."

"And if it doesn't work out?"

Reed looked out the window and for a brief moment imagined life without Kate, without her smile, without her courage. His chest emptied of joy, and he leaned back in his chair, hollow.

"Then I don't think an internship will help," he said.

Dr. Caldin smiled and relented with a nod. "In case I don't get the chance to say it, I'm glad I got to be your advisor. Your thesis is brilliant and inventive, and I look forward to watching your career."

"Thank you, Dr. Caldin, for everything."

He stood and offered his hand, which Reed accepted. Then Reed departed and made his way to his car, considering what he'd chosen. When Dr. Dickson had assured him that New York was all but guaranteed, he'd been elated. Now he'd effectively given up tickets to the Super Bowl to attend a game at the local rec center. But he couldn't be happier.

He reached the parking lot and ascended the steps to the third level. Then he made his way to his car and came to a halt. He frowned and turned around, wondering if he'd left his car somewhere else. He walked up and down the row before returning to the empty spot, certain that it had contained his car an hour ago.

His car was gone.

Chapter 2

Reed scanned the parking garage, his surprise flickering to anger. His car was a pile of junk that just happened to have an engine, requiring nearly as much oil as gas to stay mobile. Why would someone steal his wreck?

A flutter of white drew his eye to the concrete wall. He frowned and advanced to find a note taped to the concrete by a piece of tape. When he spotted his name on the card he pulled it off the wall and read the note.

On my first bad date, his car was impounded and we had to wait two hours for a tow truck.

Reed grinned as he realized the note was from Kate, and that she'd taken his car. After all their talk of bad dates he'd thought their next date would be filled with stories, but apparently Kate had decided to plan an actual bad date. He pulled out his phone but his own car rolled into view and Kate poked her head out the window.

"I'll only make you wait two minutes," she said with a smile.

Dressed in grungy clothes, her hair in disarray, and dirt on her face, she looked terrible except for the wide smile on her face. He shook his head and strode to her, and she climbed out to kiss him. Then she grinned and pointed to the passenger seat.

"Your bad date starts now," she said. "If you're up for it."

"What, now?" he asked. "You're two days early."

"One of my dates thought spontaneity was the hallmark of a good boyfriend," she said.

"That doesn't sound so bad."

"In the middle of a movie he started a popcorn fight and got us kicked out."

Reed laughed. "I once had a girl eat the gum she found under the table."

Kate grimaced. "That's disgusting."

"That's what I said."

She grinned and pointed to the passenger seat. "Get in. It's going to be a fun night of terribleness."

"When you put it that way, how can I refuse?" He circled the car and climbed into the passenger seat, excited at the prospect of a spontaneous date. "I assume tonight is going to be a bad date?"

"We've had so many great nights I figured it was time for a bad one," she said.

"And the clothes?" he asked, pointing to the rips in her jeans.

"I had a guy arrive dressed like this," she said. "Right down to the dirt on his face. I found out the next day he had lice." She shuddered. "I was really glad I didn't hold his hand."

"How old were you?" he asked.

"Fifteen," she said. "Francis was the fifth guy to ask me out and I didn't know I could say no."

"You can certainly say no," he said. "And why are we taking my car?"

"I got your spare key from Jackson," she said. "And I couldn't very well take my car, it's too nice. I once had a date show up on a bike."

"Really?" he asked.

"His car was in the shop but he didn't cancel."

Reed was laughing. "What did he expect, for you to ride on the back?"

"Actually, yes."

"You've dated some real winners."

Kate grinned and reached for a small towel which she used to wipe her face. Then she pulled her hair into a ponytail while they waited at a light. Checking herself in the mirror, she made a few finishing touches and then caught Reed watching.

"I couldn't very well go on a date looking like that."

"I thought it was rather cute," he said.

She pursed her lips and then returned her attention to the road as the light changed. "Don't tell me you like the grunge look."

"Maybe not all the time," he said. "But a girl who isn't afraid to get dirty is very attractive."

"Don't get attached," she said. "And get ready for our game."

"I assume we're telling stories of our bad dates?"

"Of course," she said. "We've talked about it before but never got around to doing it. Now I'm excited at the chance to beat you soundly."

"Is that how tonight is going to go?" he asked. "I once had a date yell at me for ten minutes because I opened her door."

"Really?"

"She thought a woman was quite capable of opening her own door."

"I guess every girl has her hot buttons."

"So what are yours?" he asked, glancing her way.

"You just want me to say them?"

"Why not?" he asked.

She shrugged and cast him a challenging look. "You first."

Reed cocked his head to the side to consider the question, and then said, "I hate it when someone leaves a wet towel on the floor."

"Does Jackson do that?"

"He used to," Reed said.

"I hate it when guys send me their nudes."

Reed grimaced. "Does that happen often?"

"More often than you'd think," she said. "There are some girls that might want it, but in my experience, most find it really irritating."

He grinned and she pulled into traffic, threading her way around campus toward the main road. The spontaneity marked a shift from past dates and he kept glancing her way, excited at discovering a new side to his girlfriend.

"I hate watching professional sports," she said. "College sports are fine, but I can't stand pro football."

They pulled into a Chick-Fil-A and she turned into the drive-through. He realized that fast food was going to be their dinner and raised an eyebrow to Kate. She turned to him with an expectant smile.

"Guy took you to McDonalds for dinner?" he guessed.

"More than one guy did that," she said. "Drive-through fast food when you're dressed up is a real mood killer."

"I assume this was in high school?"

"And college," she said. "I figured we'd replace McDonalds with Chick-Fil-A today. It's still fast food, but it's a significant upgrade."

"Amen to that," he said, ordering the spicy chicken deluxe. His choice caused Kate to raise her eyebrow.

"What?" he said defensively. "I like a little bit of spice."

"I didn't realize you liked spicy foods," she said.

"To a point," he said. "But no jalapeños."

She ordered her own meal and she found a parking spot where they could eat. They'd arrived prior to the dinner rush and the line quickly grew around the restaurant. Reed savored his sandwich and sipped his lemonade.

"This is wonderful," he said, the words muffled through the food.

"Our bad date is wonderful?" she asked.

"Fast food or fine dining," he said. "With you, everything is an adventure."

She laughed and picked up a fry. "Your turn to share a bad date. And make it a good one."

"A dance in high school," he said. "It was girl's choice and she arrived dressed in a 1930s wedding dress with a lace heart over her chest."

Kate snorted into her drink, spilling lemonade down her chin. "Really?"

"Yep," he said. "I thought she was a little strange but she seemed fun so I agreed to go. But that's not the best part. During the date she kept tripping over the dress because it was too long, so she borrowed some scissors and cut the bottom six inches off the dress."

"No," Kate breathed. "She just sliced it off?"

"And stuffed the unwanted part into the garbage can."

Kate laughed and pointed a fry at him. "Could have been worse."

"How could it have been worse?"

"She could have cut herself and you would have had to take her to the hospital."

He inclined his head in agreement and gestured to her. She took a moment to collect her thoughts, and then said, "I went on a date with a guy that seemed normal. We went to a movie but he didn't want any popcorn."

"That's not uncommon."

"I found out why at dinner," she said. "When he got to the restaurant he said he only ate meat."

"It's a lifestyle choice," he said with a smile.

"He ate a bloody steak while I had pasta and salad. I kept wondering if he would turn into a werewolf and decide the steak wasn't rare enough. And he kept talking with juice on his chin. I couldn't get over it and declined the next time he asked me out."

"I had a girl give me stitches," he said.

"Really?"

He pointed to his face, where a faint scar creased into his eyebrow. "We went ice skating and she panicked when someone bumped her. She threw me down instead and my face hit the ice. Got nine stitches."

"Sounds painful."

"She told me in the hospital that she wanted to date my friend."

She winced. "Sounds more painful."

He laughed and took a bite of his sandwich, gesturing to her to indicate it was her turn to share. Instead, she finished the last bite of her sandwich and then put the car into gear. A moment later she drove out of the lot. Turning onto the road, she pointed to the theatre around the corner.

"We need to hurry or we're going to miss the movie."

"Fast food and a movie?" he asked. "How romantic."

She smiled wryly. "I've gone on plenty of movie dates so I've got a lot of material."

"I don't think I'm winning this game," he said wryly.

"No," she replied. "You're not. But you've won the award for best dates. The least I can do is win the award for the worst."

"So you admit I won our dating challenge."

"I'm not going to admit that," she said, "but on Ember's blog, you're the clear favorite."

"At least you took second place."

She burst into a laugh and playfully hit his arm. "It doesn't count when there are just two of us."

"Maybe," he reasoned. "But it's still doing well. You should be proud."

She shook her head in chagrin. "It doesn't help that my mother is voting for you on Ember's blog. She's gotten all her friends involved."

"Most parents do like me," he said.

Her eyes sparkled mischievously as she pulled into the lot and parked. Then she pulled out a tablet. "I hope so."

He frowned. "What do you mean?"

"One of my worst movie dates included the guy's mom, who insisted on sitting between us. She kept making snide comments about me wanting her boy, who kept leering at me." She turned on the tablet and navigated to Skype. "We can't have my mom here, but I thought it only fitting that she make an appearance."

Kate's mom answered on the second ring and smiled at Reed. "Hello, Reed, it's nice to finally meet you . . ."

Chapter 3

"Mrs. Williams," Reed said with a smile. "You've been very helpful on the dating challenge."

"It's been my pleasure," she said. "And please, call me Lisa."

Kate's mother looked much like her daughter in features, and they shared the same striking green eyes. Lisa's hair was blonde, suggesting Kate had gotten her brown from her father. The roots showed a hint of grey but the rest appeared to have been dyed.

"Your daughter has your beauty," he said. "And your eyes."

The woman laughed lightly. "Kate said you were handsome, but the pictures on Ember's blog don't do you justice."

"Kate said that?" he asked, glancing her way.

"I admit nothing," Kate said, her eyes sparkling with amusement.

"I'm glad to see you two together," Lisa said. "After everything, I admit I was worried. I'm sorry for everything you went through, by the way."

"Kate was kind enough to forgive our breakup," Reed said, raising a hand to forestall Kate's interruption.

"But you weren't dating," Lisa said.

"Exactly," Reed replied.

Lisa laughed again. "How is your current date going?"

"Badly," Reed lamented. "But I think that's how it's supposed to go."

"We're revisiting all our bad dates," Kate said, leaning into the frame. "Remember?"

"We've all had our share," Lisa said. "I once had a guy try to grope me—at church."

"Really?" Reed asked, aghast.

"Mom!" Kate exclaimed, and shuddered. "That's not the type of thing I want to hear."

"What?" Lisa protested. "It's not like I'm showing him pictures of you naked in the tub or anything. I have them, by the way . . ."

"*Mom!*" Kate said, flushing. "You're not supposed to make this an *actual* bad date."

"Kid pictures would be great," Reed said brightly, and Kate cast him a scathing look.

Lisa smiled and motioned to him. "Your mother has already sent me plenty from when you were a child. They're simply adorable."

"What?" he asked, caught off guard. "You've talked to my mom?"

"Kate didn't tell you?" Lisa asked innocently. "She gave me your mom's number and we've become good friends over the last few weeks. Do tell her I said hello."

Reed looked to Kate but she was fighting not to laugh, her hand clamped over her mouth in an attempt to keep the amusement from bursting free. Reed glared at her and then returned his attention to the screen.

"Can you include pictures of the guys Kate has dated?" he asked. "And their nicknames?"

"I think that's enough," Kate said with a strangled sound. "We do have a movie to get to."

She tried to grab the iPad but Lisa called out, "Wait, there is one more thing I wanted to ask."

"Is it going to embarrass me?" Kate asked warily.

"Not everything is about you," Lisa said. "I found out yesterday that Bake's deployment ends the week after Thanksgiving, so we're doing our holiday in early December. Tyler and Orin will be there as well. Think you can you make it?"

"Let me know the dates and I will," she said.

"What about you, Reed?" Lisa turned her gaze to him. "Would you like to join us for Thanksgiving?"

"Mom," Kate said, exasperated. "Can you let me do the inviting?"

"At the rate you're going, I'd be lucky to meet him in the next decade. Reed?"

"Your daughter has proven herself to be quite bold," Reed said. "If she invites me to your family holiday, I'll see what I can do."

"Kate?" Lisa asked.

"Goodbye, mother," Kate said.

"But I haven't—"

Kate ended the call and sighed. "I'm sorry. I didn't know she was going to ask that. Sometimes she can be manipulative."

"I think that's a mother's prerogative," he said.

"We don't want to be late to the movie," she said.

Obviously unsettled by the conversation, she checked the time and stashed the tablet in its case. Then they left the car and walked to the theatre. After purchasing tickets for an animated film, they grabbed popcorn and slushies and found seats in the center of the theatre. The movie had been out for a few months and the theatre was empty.

"I really am sorry," she finally said.

"Because of the invite?" he asked. "Do you not want me to come?"

"I do," she said hastily. "But I think she planned that to make you feel like you had to say yes."

"What if I want to meet your family?"

"Would you?" she asked.

"Why not?" he asked. "I'd like to meet your brothers."

"Are you saying you want to go to Arizona with me?"

"I don't know," he said. "I haven't been invited yet." He smiled and grabbed the popcorn.

"Would you like to come home with me for Thanksgiving?" she asked.

"I thought you'd never ask," he said.

She laughed and threw a piece of popcorn at him. He protested and threw one back, but before the war could escalate a woman and her young son entered and found seats. Reed and Kate exchanged a look and by unspoken accord called it a tie. A moment later the previews began.

Although the conversation had lightened, Reed sensed a shift. Even if the invite had been coerced by Lisa, spending a holiday with a girlfriend implied a seriousness to their relationship that went beyond dating. As if realizing the same thing, Kate was quiet for the first half of the movie.

"It's your turn," he finally whispered.

"For what?"

"Another story of a bad date," he murmured.

She took a sip of her drink and smiled. "I had a guy take me to a horror movie at a nasty old theatre."

"Do you like horror movies?"

"Hate 'em," she said. "I covered my eyes most of the time and then afterward he wanted to comfort me in the back seat."

"Sounds like a real winner," he said.

"The worst part? He 'forgot' his wallet, so I had to pay."

"You paid for a terrible date?"

"I didn't feel like I had a choice."

He was already holding her hand so he squeezed it. "That's terrible."

"It wasn't all bad," she whispered. "We had seafood for dinner— which I also had to pay for—and I got sick. That and the movie made me throw up in his car. Only time I've ever been grateful for vomit."

He smothered a laugh and glanced at the woman with her son, who appeared annoyed. As they enjoyed the movie, he wracked his brain for how he could top such a terrible date. Before he could, the woman glanced his way again.

"I think we're annoying our friends," he whispered, using his chin to point to them.

"We can suspend the game until the end of the movie," she said. "It will give you time to come up with ideas."

"I don't need the time," he protested.

She smiled. "I think you do."

The woman cast them another annoyed look and they shared a grin. Reed settled in to enjoy the rest of the movie. Although the theatre was the cheap kind that showed movies months after they'd come out, it was mostly clean and the seats were moderately comfortable.

When the credits rolled he leaned over to her. "I enjoyed the movie."

"Not too childish?" she asked.

"No," he replied, leaning over to kiss her. "I enjoyed it."

"Liar," she said, rising to her feet.

"You don't believe me?" he asked. "I really liked the first one. It's my favorite Disney movie."

"Plus they have powers."

"Always a bonus," he said with a smile.

They dropped their trash and left the theatre behind. As had already become a habit, he reached out and took her hand, pleased that it still sent a thrill into his chest. She glanced his way and their eyes met, her smile turning soft.

"As much as I loved the popcorn," he said, "I hope dessert is in our future."

"Oh it is," she said, and her smile turned mischievous. "But I don't think you're going to like it . . ."

Chapter 4

"Please tell me it's not fast food fish," he said. "I don't want to throw up in your car."

She laughed and shook her head. "It's so much worse."

"Do tell."

They climbed into the car and she left the parking lot. "One of my early dates took me to a movie. Afterward I said I was hungry so he said we could get something at his work because he had a discount."

"I'm getting a bad feeling about this," he said. "Where did he work?"

"A gas station."

He cringed. "He took you to dinner . . . at a gas station?"

"It's as bad as it sounds," she said. "It wasn't a nice one. It was this dirty, hole-in-the wall place at the edge of Phoenix."

"What did you eat?"

"Chips, crackers, and a hot dog that had probably been on the heater for months." She shuddered. "It was terrible."

"So I take it we're going to a gas station for dessert?"

"We are," she said. "But I won't do you the disservice of taking you to a nasty gas station. We're going to a nice one. There's a 7-11 where we'll have to figure out a nice treat."

"You don't already have a plan?"

"My date to the gas station walked in and asked me what I wanted. He said it like it was an all you can eat buffet."

"So now we get to choose?"

"I hope you can surprise me," she said.

"It's what I live for," he said.

As they drove to the gas station they took a break from the bad date game and talked about their fall semester. He marveled about how much he craved the mundane details of her life. The engineering building and the psychology building were on different sides of campus, so they rarely saw each other during the day. Two days a week they were able to meet for lunch and he looked forward to those moments, but they never seemed to satiate his desire for more time.

"I wish we had more time together," he said, voicing his thoughts. "Over the summer our classes lined up pretty well, but this semester is the opposite."

"I feel the same way," she said. "But in a way I like it."

"Getting tired of me already?" he asked, indignant.

"It's just nice to be wanted," she said.

He laughed and gestured to campus. "So it's not just me that wants more time?"

"No," she said, her eyes soft. "I wish we had more too."

"Don't worry," he said. "We only have a few months and then I'll be done with school. We can have more time in the spring."

"How's it going with the internships?"

Her question was said casually, but a current of worry had appeared in her voice. "Dr. Caldin found two internships I can apply for. I'll have to wait a few weeks but my chances are decent."

"What if you don't get in?" she asked.

She was obviously trying to keep it from showing, but the worry had deepened. He leaned over to kiss her on the cheek. "I'm not going anywhere, Kate."

She smiled and glanced his way. "Are you sure this isn't moving too fast? You really don't have to come to my family's Thanksgiving. It's not even on the actual holiday."

"Is it usually like that?" he asked.

"Holidays have always been flexible in my family," she said. "First it was my dad, and then when Bake and Tyler joined the military it was even harder. Now my dad's retired, so it isn't as hard to line up a day when everyone is on leave."

"I really would like to meet your family," he said. "After talking so much with your mom to plan our other dates, I'd like to meet her so she doesn't think I'm a stalker boyfriend."

"That's not how she sees you," she said.

"Then how does she see me?"

She shook her head. "You're dodging the question."

"So are you."

She laughed. "Seriously. Do you think we're moving too fast?"

"All I know is that I crave time with you," he said.

"Really?"

"Don't sound so surprised," he said. "Have I not made that clear with the abundance of calls and showing up every day? It's a wonder you haven't told me you needed a break."

"We tried that," she said. "I didn't like it so much."

He grinned. "I vastly prefer being together."

She pulled into the gas station and parked. Then she turned to meet his gaze, an earnest smile on her face. "I feel the same way," she said.

"I was hoping you'd say that," he said. "Because otherwise our gas station treat would be really awkward."

She laughed and they got out of the car. Entering the mini-mart of the gas station, he scanned the interior of the structure, grateful it looked clean and orderly. It was not overly large but it wasn't small either.

The counter was situated to the left while the bank of slushies and sodas sat on the back wall. Aisles extended to the right and the outside wall contained the refrigerated drinks. It carried that odd sense of familiarity that all gas stations possessed, as if he'd been in that exact one before but had forgotten because they all looked the same. The bored woman behind the counter did not look up from her magazine, so Reed walked down the first aisle.

"We have gourmet cookies by chef Nestle," she said. "Or other sugar-injected confections."

"So many options," he said. "What will we choose?"

"My date tried to buy beer," she said, gesturing to the coolers. "His boss just laughed at him."

"That would be embarrassing," he said.

"He was," she replied, and then glanced his way. "You know, I assumed you didn't drink because of your dad. But is it because of what happened to Aura?"

"Both," he said with a nod. "My dad was a heavy drinker for my entire childhood. It wasn't until after I left home that he got into AA. Then Tim nearly killed Aura, and I swore I'd never drink."

"So you've never tasted alcohol?"

"To be honest I'm afraid to," he said. "When I was in grade school a kid made fun of my dad and said drunks ran in the family. He claimed I would end up just like him. I learned that alcoholism can be hereditary so I vowed never to touch it."

"I bet that took courage."

Reed shrugged and recalled all the times he'd heard his dad stumble in the door after a night at his favorite bar. He'd never beaten Reed's mom, as far as he knew, but he'd been a slovenly mess, sometimes just passing out on the floor because he couldn't make it up the stairs.

"It's easy to say no before you start," he said.

"So the wine selection is not on the menu," she said, waving to the refrigerated doors. "But that still leaves the carbon dioxide and glucose infused water."

"You mean the sodas?"

"That's what I said."

He spotted a package of circus peanuts and picked it up. "Now this is a perfect dessert," he said. "Sweet taste, delicious texture, and a nice aftertaste that lingers with you."

"Very astute," she said sagely. "But I prefer the more robust Take Five. Imported chocolate, hand drizzled over a pretzel baked over a wood fire. Perfect with a touch of caramel and sea salt."

He couldn't take it anymore and laughed, then she broke down as well. The woman at the counter looked up at them, her eyes registering curiosity before returning to the magazine. Unable to resist the description, he picked up the Take Five and used it to point at Kate.

"You should be in advertising," he said.

"I just like them," she said smugly, picking up one for herself. "Drink?"

"I don't think I can take you describing the Gatorade as 'pure volcanic spring water blended with melted glacial ice and organic flavors unique to the Amazon jungle'."

"I was going to say let's get Slurpees," she said. "Blue raspberry, of course."

"Deal," he said.

They filled their drinks and Kate paid for their treat. The girl hardly looked up as she mechanically ran the register, accepting Kate's credit card and then handing it back. When she was done the woman lapsed back into her previous stupor of magazine reading.

"Your dessert menu is excellent," Reed said.

The girl looked up and stared, and Kate smothered a laugh. Reed merely grinned and walked out the door, where they both burst out laughing. Back in the car, they used their Styrofoam cups to toast the evening and opened the treats. As Reed savored the dessert, Kate gestured to him.

"You've had plenty of time to think about your worst dates," she said. "But I'm leaving you in the dust. I hope you have some good ones left."

"Don't worry," he said with a smile. "I've saved the best for last."

Chapter 5

"Let's hear it," Kate said, sipping her Slurpee.

"My first year at college—before I started the creative dating—I met a girl at a school event. I thought she was a student, but she was wearing a formal dress, which I found odd."

"What was the event?"

"I think it was a fall social," he said. "She came up to me and just started talking, and wouldn't stop. She really set me on edge but I couldn't explain why, so I said I had to meet some friends and escaped. But she followed me into the crowd. I only managed to lose her because she couldn't fit through the crowd in her large dress."

"That's it?" Kate asked. "You'll have to do better than that."

"I haven't even gotten to the good part," he said. "When the social was ending I spotted her approaching and tried to hide behind the refreshments table, where a friend of mine was working at the punch bowl."

Kate snorted, nearly spilling Slurpee down her shirt. "You hid from a girl?"

"I told you she gave me a really weird feeling," he protested.

"I still can't believe you ran and hid."

"It wasn't like that," he said, and then shrugged in chagrin. "Maybe a little. She tracked me down and put an arm around me, and said she needed someone to walk her to her car . . . for safety reasons."

"You can't refuse that," she said, her eyes sparkling with amusement.

"I didn't," Reed said. "My friend said he had to help clean up after the social and bailed, so I reluctantly walked her to her car. Twenty steps out the door she said—in her exact words—*I'm looking for a guy*."

"She actually said that?"

He nodded. "Turns out she wasn't a student at all. She just went to the socials and bars hunting for a husband. She had money from her family and didn't need college or a job, so she was a professional manhunter."

"What did you say?"

"I claimed I was considering doing volunteer work out of the country."

"You lied to her?" Kate asked.

"Not exactly," he said. "I'd gotten a flyer about it early that day and actually considered it. I didn't say the trip was nine months away."

"How did she take it?"

Reed cringed at the memory. "She said, and I quote, 'That's okay. When you get back, maybe we can get married'."

Kate spit Slurpee onto her shirt, and coughed as blue ice dripped down her chin. Grabbing a napkin she'd been using as a plate, she wiped her mouth, still laughing.

"She's bold, I give her that."

"I almost ran," he said. "Just bolted like I was in a race for my life."

"She couldn't catch you in her dress," she reasoned.

"Exactly," he replied.

"And you'd already proven a willingness to run from her before."

"That's not really what you're supposed to get from this story," he said, frowning.

She wiped tears of laughter from her eyes. "Was she pretty?"

"Let's just say she wasn't my type," he replied.

"So did you run?"

"I figured it would hurt her too much, so I claimed I had to pick up a friend. She asked for my number but I said I didn't have a phone. She said she could give me hers but I was already walking away. I told her maybe I'd see her at another social and kept walking."

Kate was laughing again, tears streaming down her cheeks as she struggled to keep her drink from spilling. "Stop," she said. "I can't take any more."

He grinned and shook his head. "The last thing she said was, 'but I have a nice car'."

Kate leveled an accusing finger at him. "She treated you like an arrogant guy treats a girl."

"What?"

She nodded. "Think about it. She thought because she had money and a car that she deserved attention."

"Guys don't propose ten minutes after meeting a girl," he said.

"That's not true," she said. "I had a friend consent to pity coffee. That night the guy showed up with flowers, and kept talking about how their meeting was destiny. He kept leaving notes for her and two days later showed up at her work in a tux and bearing a ring."

"You've got to be kidding."

"I'm not," she said. "She said no and he was crushed for months."

"When was this?"

"Freshman year," she said.

"That can't happen very often," he protested.

"More often than you'd think," she said. "Sometimes guys get really attached and become blind to signs of rejection."

"That ever happen to you?"

"Not a proposal," she said. "But close. In high school I had a guy in my geography class change his schedule so he could sit next to me in every class. He told everyone we were planning on getting married after graduation. We never even went on a date."

"He just said you were getting married?"

"I don't think he meant to," she said. "He made a claim to a friend and it kind of spiraled from there. But he didn't back down when it blew up. The next week he walked into class and tried to kiss me."

"And?"

"Remember what I did to Mr. Barris from the dancing class?"

He recalled how the old man had tried to grab her backside, and she'd slapped him. "You slapped the kid?" he asked.

"I slugged him."

He laughed at the image of the poor guy. "I hope he got the hint."

"He never bothered me again," she said. "But I still feel bad. He just wanted to feel wanted."

"Some guys take the opposite approach," he said. "I once left a bracelet on a girl's desk. Never told her it was me."

"So?"

"So guys have no clue how to talk to girls," he said. "You're all fascinating and gorgeous and we get a little crazy whenever we look in your eyes."

"So you were like that?"

"All the way until I was eighteen," he said. "I think all guys have to go through this phase, but some take decades to grow out of it."

"You make it sound like it's a rite of passage."

"Learning to not be stupid?" he asked. "It is."

She smiled and finished her Slurpee. Then she gestured to the clock. "I'd better get you home. It's getting late."

"I've really enjoyed the bad date," he said.

"Me too," she replied. "But we both know I won."

"Did you not hear my last story?" he asked.

"Doesn't count," she said smugly. "You weren't on a date."

He opened his mouth to protest but there was no room for disagreement. He chuckled in chagrin, realizing that he could not beat her in a bad date competition. He'd had the benefit of choosing his dates, while she'd been at the mercy of whoever extended an invitation.

He considered sharing his truly difficult dates, like when a girl told him that if he didn't ask her out again she would commit suicide, or the one that had cut herself every night. But looking back he realized the girls' problems didn't mean they were bad dates, it just meant they needed help.

"You win," he conceded.

"About time," she said.

They got out to drop their empty cups in the trash and then took a picture in front of the gas station. Ember had insisted they continue to chronicle each date with a photo, even though they were already together. As the flash blinded him, Reed wondered if Kate would ever go on a bad date again.

They returned to the car and she drove him home, but kept her speed low as if reluctant to drop him off. When they did arrive in the driveway she got out and opened his door, and then walked him to his porch.

"Kissing you goodbye is significantly better than a hug," he said.

He pulled her in and leaned into the kiss, the warmth of the contact flooding his frame. Her body seemed to wrap into his, fitting like two puzzle pieces. When they parted he reached up and threaded a stray hair behind her ear.

"A bad date with you is better than a great date with anyone else."

"Really?"

"Always," he said.

She went up on her toes and kissed him again. "I look forward to your next invite."

"It will come," he said. "See you tomorrow?"

"And the next day," she replied.

He kissed her again and then reluctantly let her go. She seemed to want to linger but turned and strode to her car. As the car backed out she waved, but as had become tradition, he remained on the porch until she was out of sight. Then he sighed and opened his door, already wondering what his next date would be.

Chapter 6

He stepped into the house and found Jackson sprawled across the couch, asleep. Shelby sat with his head in her lap, texting on her phone. She looked up at his entry and made a quieting motion toward Jackson. Then she extricated herself and walked into the kitchen.

"How was his game?" Reed murmured, recalling that it was his first in the fall intramural program.

"Triple overtime," she said. "He missed a shot that could have won the game."

"He lost?" Reed asked. Normally Jackson's team did very well.

"They played an old rival," Shelby said, picking up the fortune cookie from what had evidently been their dinner. "He was pretty bummed and fell asleep shortly after we got back. How was your bad date?"

"Did she get any ideas from you?" Reed asked.

Shelby nodded and motioned vaguely toward the theatre. "I suggested the movie."

"It was fun," he said, and then smiled. "For a bad date."

She smothered a laugh, but a stirring on the couch indicated Jackson had heard it. He appeared in the doorway and padded into the kitchen like a lumbering bear. Spotting Reed, he came to a halt and yawned.

"When did you get home?"

"A few minutes ago," Reed said. "Sorry to wake you up."

"I didn't think we would," Shelby said, patting him on the back. "You snored like you were in a coma." Her expression turned stricken and she looked to Reed. "Sorry, I forgot about Aura."

Reed shook his head. "Aura is gone," he said. "There's nothing I can do about that. Besides, I'm really enjoying things with Kate."

Jackson slapped him on the shoulder, almost knocking him into the fridge. "At least things are working out for you. My game was—"

"I already told him," Shelby said.

Jackson grunted and grabbed a beer from the fridge. Then he trudged to the table and sank into a chair. He stared morosely at the bottle without taking a drink until Reed poked him in the ribs.

"Hey!" he protested.

"Come on," he said. "Let's go buy some cold cereal."

"What, now?" he asked. "It's after midnight."

"Are you turning down cold cereal?" Reed challenged.

He snorted. "Never. Shelby? You coming?"

"Are you asking me out to Walmart? To buy cold cereal?"

"Yes?" His expression turned hopeful.

She grinned and reached for her purse. "How can I refuse such a romantic?"

"See why I love this woman?" Jackson asked, kissing her before disappearing to retrieve his sneakers.

"He's so easy to please," Shelby said in an aside.

Reed smothered a laugh and a moment later they piled into Jackson's truck. The quest had alleviated Jackson's funk, to a degree, and they talked about the game and Reed's date. Shelby shared several of her worst dates and Jackson chimed in.

"I suppose everyone has had them," Shelby said. "Did you ever take Aura on a date?"

Realizing he had never told Shelby the whole story, Reed briefly related the date they'd been on when she'd turned him down and left with Tim. Shelby grimaced as he described watching Tim drive away.

"That's brutal," she said. "And the accident was a week later?"

"It was," Reed said, looking out the window but seeing Tim driving away.

They pulled into the Walmart and Jackson parked near the front. As they walked inside Reed looked to the sky, which had darkened considerably since his date. The air heralded a bite that signified the approaching winter.

"Every guy has experienced a brutal rejection," Jackson said sagely.

"You?" Reed scoffed. "You're built like a superhero. When was the last time you were rejected?"

"Second grade," Jackson lamented. "Candace Wilderbell said she wouldn't hold my hand because I had meat for a head."

"She called you a meathead?" Shelby asked, laughing.

"I think she heard it from an older sibling but didn't say it right. Didn't matter. I tried to push her down but she had arms as big as the tire swing. It was my first split lip outside of sports."

The nostalgic tone caused Reed and Shelby to exchange a look and laugh. Then they walked into the store and headed to the cereal aisle. Reed's phone buzzed and he pulled it out, pleased to find a message from Kate.

"Kate?" Shelby guessed.

"She got home a few minutes ago but then left. Said her roommates needed to get something for tomorrow."

"Where'd they go?" Shelby asked.

"Right here," Jackson said.

They turned down the cereal aisle and Reed looked up. Standing in the middle of the aisle were Kate with all three of her roommates, all in pajamas. Reed shoved his phone into his pocket and walked to her, delighted at the surprise. He wrapped her into a hug and kissed her soundly, eliciting smiles and whistles.

"What are you doing here?" he asked.

"It's my fault," Brittney said. "I needed sugar for the cookies I was making."

"And I suggested we just go to the store," Ember said. Then her eyes fell on Jackson. "What's with the rumpled clothes?"

"I fell asleep," he said, indignant.

"Because you lost your game?" Ember asked.

He grumbled under his breath and looked to Shelby, who grinned helplessly. "It's not my fault. I texted my friends."

"We're your friends too, meathead," Ember said. "And you could have told us about the game but you—why are you all laughing?"

Reed, Jackson, and Shelby were all in fits but Reed managed to say, "A story for another time."

Confused, Kate shrugged and leaned close. "I'm glad to find you here."

"Me too," he said. "I didn't really want to say goodbye."

"What did you need from the store?" Marta asked.

"Dinner supplies," Jackson said.

"Cereal?" Brittney asked.

Jackson sniffed. "You don't need to sound so condescending. You like to cook. I like to let General Mills do the cooking for me."

Reed watched his friends talk to Kate's roommates. The group was an odd mixture of personalities and types. Ember was dressed in full-length pajamas that sported unicorns and rainbows. Jackson wore basketball shorts and an old t-shirt with a basketball, and he towered over the redhead.

Marta and Brittney wore flannel and long shirts, while Shelby was also dressed in basketball shorts and an exercise shirt. Despite their differences, the five friends talked like they had been together for ages, and Reed overheard Ember and Shelby talking about Ember joining Shelby's basketball team.

"We could use a point guard with fire," Shelby was saying. "Do you play?"

"She'll just get you technical fouls," Jackson warned.

Ember casually flicked her finger on his arm. "I leave my anger off the court," she said. "Most of the time."

Kate leaned over to Reed and lowered her voice. "Is it just me, or are they really weird friends?"

"They *are* really weird friends," he said, smiling as he listened to them debate Ember's anger on a basketball court. "But they somehow work."

"I never thought our challenge would bring them together," Reed said.

"I never thought it would do a lot of things," Kate said, leaning up to kiss him.

"I'm getting the milk," Jackson said. "You can pick the cereal."

As he walked away Reed's phone buzzed and he pulled it out. He glanced at the screen and frowned, surprised at the caller. Kate asked who it was, but he shook his head and showed her the screen and the Miami area code.

"Miami?" she asked. "Aura's parents?"

He shrugged and put the phone to his ear. He said hello but his greeting was met with silence, causing him to frown in confusion. Several moments passed until a young voice spoke his name.

"Reed?"

He froze, the blood draining from his face. Kate saw his response and guessed the truth, her features going ashen. Marta noticed first and nudged Brittney, and one by one the others fell silent. Then Ember pointed to Reed.

"Is someone dead?" she asked Kate.

Kate shook her head and spoke into the stillness. "The opposite. Aura's awake."

Volume 17: The Marathon Date

Chapter 1

Kate stared at Reed, her emotions in turmoil. They still stood in the store, all crowded around Reed in the cereal aisle. She was highly aware of the sound of his voice, of the tightness to his expression, the hope. He talked in muted tones with Aura, the girl he'd loved, the girl that had been in a coma for three years, the girl Kate had thought squarely in his past.

Until now.

She was relieved Aura was awake. Withering away in a coma because of a drunk driver was a terrible fate that she wouldn't wish on anyone. For Aura to wake up was a miracle that should be celebrated.

But this was Aura, the girl Reed had loved for three years, his unrequited affection and her accident leaving an indelible scar on Reed's heart. Kate had nearly lost him because of his promise to Aura, and now she was back. Would he go back to her? Would he want to be with her? How would it change his feelings . . .

Reed's hand touched hers, their fingers intertwining. Their eyes met and he gave a tiny nod, warming the knot in her chest. In the midst of what was likely the second hardest phone call of his life, Reed recognized Kate's fear.

"I'm glad to hear that," he said to Aura, but he squeezed Kate's hand, his eyes never leaving hers.

Relief trickled through her frame and she allowed a small smile. She could see the pain, the worry, the relief, written on his features, and there was a stillness about his body, like he wanted to shout and run or drop to his knees and cry. He did neither.

"I'll talk to you soon," he finally said, and hung up.

He stared at his phone, the rest of them all standing around like a bomb had just detonated. Kate vaguely heard someone ask where to find the nuts but none of them looked, and the woman walked away, casting strange looks at them.

"I can't believe it," Reed said.

"When did she wake up?" Kate found herself asking, her voice distant, like someone else was speaking.

"Three weeks ago," Reed said. "Sheila wanted to call me but Aura wanted to wait until she could tell me herself."

"Is she going to be okay?" Brittney asked.

"She's starting physical therapy," Reed said, still staring at the phone. "They think another couple of weeks and she might be able to walk."

Kate noticed her roommates kept looking at her, their expressions betraying their worry as they glanced back to Reed, who still seemed frozen. Kate couldn't blame him, but each passing second she felt the distance grow between them.

"Sorry," he said, shaking himself and finally looking up. "It's just a lot to take in. Kate, are you okay?"

His blue eyes fell upon her, and although there was a weight behind them, there was also concern. He turned so he faced her, bringing them close. His effort eased her concern but the tightness in her chest remained, like bands of steel constricting her breathing.

"It's you I'm worried about," Kate said.

"How did she wake up?" Marta asked.

"The doctors are still trying to figure it out, but they think a new stimulus acted like a catalyst for her brain."

Kate exchanged a worried look with Marta, her expression indicating they were thinking the same thing. The only new stimulus had been when Reed showed up at the hospital four weeks ago. Had his appearance woken her? It seemed absurd, but she couldn't bring herself to reject it outright.

"Are we getting cereal or not?" Jackson asked, striding up with a gallon of milk. He frowned when he caught sight of the circle crowded around Reed. "What's the deal? Did I miss something?"

"I'll explain later," Shelby said, grabbing Jackson's elbow and dragging him down the aisle. "Bye girls," she cast over her shoulder. "Reed, we'll be in the car when you're ready."

"We have a few things to grab," Marta said, giving Kate's arm a sympathetic squeeze. "We'll check out and meet you in the car."

"I'm not leaving," Ember said, folding her arms. "Anything Reed is about to say can go through me."

"Ember," Kate said, but Reed looked to the diminutive redhead, whose eyes flashed dangerously.

"I'm not going to hurt your friend," Reed said quietly.

Ember locked eyes for several seconds, and then abruptly stabbed a finger at him. "If you do, I hurt you back."

She spun on her heel and followed the girls down the hall, the unicorns and rainbows on her pajamas dancing angrily. Reed chuckled under his breath when she disappeared around the corner.

"Even wearing unicorns, the girl is intimidating."

"Those are her favorite pajamas," Kate said.

Alone in the aisle, she realized it was probably one in the morning, and they had just been on her bad date an hour ago. She grimaced and looked away, wishing she hadn't planned an actual bad date the same day Aura called.

"What was that look for?" Reed asked.

"I just took you on a terrible date on purpose," she said. "And now Aura calls."

"Are you worried?"

"Should I be?" her heart thudded against her ribs.

He lifted her chin so she looked into his eyes. "Never," he said softly. "Awake or asleep, distant or close, Aura is merely a friend from my past."

"You can't say you don't feel anything," Kate said.

"The opposite," Reed said. "I'm relieved and worried and nervous—but most of all I'm afraid for you, that you'll think this changes our relationship."

"How can it not?" Kate dared to ask.

"You don't need to be afraid," he said, wrapping his strong arms around her shoulders. "She's just a friend." He said it with a trace of amusement that made her laugh into his shoulder.

"I've heard that before," she said.

She clung to him, hoping that what he said was true, but Aura was his first love. Kate had shared a few dates with Reed. How could that stand against a ten-year friendship and three years of unrequited love?

"I can practically hear the thoughts churning in your head," he said.

"Sorry," she said. "I just can't stop comparing—"

"Wait," he said. "I've just had an idea."

Confused by his response, she tried to gauge the sudden mischief in his eyes. The weight of Aura's reappearance remained on his face, but it was now overshadowed by determination. He caught her hand and headed deeper into the store.

"Where are we going?"

"I already had the next challenge date planned," he said. "But I've just decided to tweak it. I know you're worried, and the moment we separate, your worry will just get worse."

"Is that what you think will happen?" she asked, a bit of a challenge in her voice.

He cast a look back, a smile on his face. "There's the courage I love to see. Am I wrong?"

"No," Kate said.

He led her into the camping section and came to a halt, spinning to face her. His expression had suddenly turned serious and a little nervous, causing her smile to falter. He seemed to wrestle with a choice before finally he shrugged.

"Aura wants to visit me," he said.

Her smile evaporated and she spoke woodenly. "When?"

"A few weeks. I told you so you'd have all the bad news. Now you get the good news. I'm starting our date early."

"What do you mean, early?" she asked. "The next challenge date isn't for two weeks."

"I know," he said. "But we start tonight."

She suddenly realized she was standing next to sleeping bags and raised an eyebrow. "Just what are you suggesting?"

He grinned and motioned to the nearest. "I'm suggesting a marathon date. We stick together for two entire weeks."

"And why do you need the sleeping bag?"

"So I can sleep on your living room floor," he said. "That is, if you accept the invite . . ."

Chapter 2

"You can't be serious," she said.

She scoffed at the idea even as excitement filled her chest. She'd been dreading walking away from him since the moment Aura had called, and feared the doubt that would haunt her just walking to the car, let alone when lying in bed.

"If I'm next to you, you can't possibly be worried about Aura," he said.

"But a fourteen-day date?" she asked.

"I said it was going to be a marathon date," he replied. "You think your roommates will mind?"

"If they do, I'm sure Jackson won't mind me staying at your place," Kate said.

"Does that mean it's a yes?"

She permitted a smile. "It sounds like fun."

He grabbed a sleeping bag and then paused. "Same rules apply," he warned. "I can't let you think I'm easy."

She laughed. "No one could say that about you," she said. "Ever."

He grinned and cradled the sleeping bag under one arm. As they walked to the front of the store he briefly let go of her hand to call Jackson and inform him that he'd be getting a ride with Kate, but he'd be stopping home to pack a bag. Kate could hear the amusement in Jackson's voice.

"Well played, brother," Jackson said, approvingly. "Just remember to do everything I would do."

"She can hear you," Reed said.

"Good!" Jackson said.

"I'll see you at home," Reed said, and hung up. Then he turned to Kate. "You want to warn the blondes?"

Since they were in the checkout, she sent them a quick text while Reed bought his absurdly large sleeping bag. She kept smiling at his back, excited and nervous at the prospect of spending fourteen days straight with Reed. As they walked out of the store she frowned.

"How is this going to work with classes?"

"We already agreed they aren't overlapping," he replied. "I'll just go to your classes and you can come to mine."

Her excitement mounted. "You're serious about this, aren't you?"

"Why not?" he asked. "I think it will be fun."

"Or we could get tired of each other."

He came to a stop and pulled her hand so they faced each other. "We'll be together," he said. "We'll be fine."

"You mean like breakfast and lunch and dinner and everything?"

"Everything except bathroom time," he said. "Because that would just be weird."

She laughed, the sound echoing over the empty Walmart parking lot. "A marathon date," she said. "I guess we should go for it."

They reached Ember's jeep and climbed into the back. Ember looked over her shoulder and eyed him like a criminal in a lineup, her eyes settling on the large sleeping bag on his lap. Squished between Kate and Marta, Reed merely smiled.

"Hey roomy," he said brightly.

Marta snorted a laugh and Brittney grinned, glancing at Ember before trying not to laugh. Ember merely glowered at him for several moments. Then she turned and keyed the ignition before stomping on the gas pedal and driving across several parking spots on her way out.

"You'd better not snore."

"I don't," he said. "Or at least I don't think so."

"Ember," Kate said, "if you're not okay with this . . ."

"I don't mind Reed," Ember said. "And I think it's a great idea. But I don't like Aura coming to our town."

Reed glanced at Kate and she gave an apologetic shrug. "Sorry, I told them she was coming here."

"When?" Brittney asked.

"A few weeks," Reed said. "I didn't get a day."

They stopped at his house and he packed a quick bag, stuffing clothes and a toothbrush into a small suitcase. Kate stayed with him, sitting on the bed after the blondes had left. She noticed he kept the door open, but it was still exhilarating to be in his bedroom—the first time since they were dating for real. She knew nothing was going to happen tonight, but it was one more wall coming down. It made her wonder how many walls remained . . .

"Are you doing this just because of Aura?" she asked, trying to stop thinking about his bed.

He considered the question and then shook his head. "It might have given me the idea, but now that we're doing it, I really want to finish."

"I do too," she said. "I've never heard of anyone doing something like this."

"Certainly not for two weeks," he replied.

131

He finished his bag and grabbed his backpack before they went out to his car. Jackson and Shelby stood in the doorway as he drove away and she waved to them, amused that they resembled concerned parents.

"I can't believe we're doing this," she said.

"Me either," he said, his tone tinged with excitement.

She glanced his way, gratified at how he'd turned an impossible situation into an impossible date. Reed could have said he needed time or space, or just asked Kate to leave, but he'd turned immediately to her, thinking of her. And she'd been thinking of herself. Guilt assailed her and she reached over and kissed his cheek at a stoplight.

"What was that for?" he asked.

"I'm sorry," she said. "When you got that call I couldn't stop thinking about what she could do to us . . . to me."

"Kate, I . . ."

"Don't," she said. "You responded better than I did."

"I was worried too," he admitted. "But there were just too many emotions for me to pick just one. Then I saw your face and knew what you must be feeling."

"Are you okay?" she asked. "I should have asked earlier but I'm asking now. I can't imagine what you're feeling."

"The shock is wearing off," he said. "But I still can't believe she's awake. I'd accepted the fact that she was gone a long time ago, and that call could have been that she died."

"I'm glad she's alive," Kate said, and when he looked to her in surprise she added, "The blondes and I had a talk a while ago about Aura. The truth is that Aura could have been any one of us. We've all ridden with a guy who had drunk too much and we were too afraid to say anything."

"Even Ember?"

"She wasn't always that fiery," Kate said. "That came in high school, or so I'm told."

He chuckled wryly. "I'm about to see behind the curtain, to witness women in their natural habitat. I can only imagine what I will learn—or will I be eaten alive?"

She laughed with him and then he parked on the street in front of her house. They got out and walked up to the house together, and for the first time in their relationship, entered the house together at the end of the night.

Her roommates had already blown up an air mattress and put on sheets, a welcome for which he thanked them profusely. The girls were ready for bed and Brittney yawned, apologizing as she departed for her room on the second floor. Marta followed.

Ember grinned. "I would ask if you need me to guard your door," she said. "But I'd rather he went in than stayed out."

"*Ember*," Kate said, exasperated.

"What?" Ember asked with a shrug. "Can't I want my friend to have some fun?"

She flushed. "It's not like that."

"Too bad," Ember said and walked into her bedroom.

"Sorry," Kate said.

"She's my roommate now," Reed said, amused. "I'll be fine."

It was after two but she helped Reed set up his bed. As she did the reality of what they were doing settled in, and she realized their date had already begun—and it wasn't going to end for weeks. She kept smiling, excited at the prospect of waking up and seeing him in her house, to spend every minute with him until the marathon date culminated in two weeks.

They parted briefly so she could change into her pajamas, a pair of short shorts and tank top. She returned to kiss him goodnight, an odd yet strangely intimate experience as they sat on the couch just feet from his bed.

"I'm glad we were at the store together," she murmured.

"Can you imagine if I'd gotten that call at my house?" he asked. "We wouldn't be having a sleepover right now."

"I'll thank Aura when I see her," she said with a smile.

"Good night, Kate," he said.

"Good night, Reed," she replied. "I'll see you at breakfast."

She gave him a final, lingering kiss and then returned to her bedroom, glancing back as she slipped inside. Already dressed for bed, she climbed under the blanket and lay down, unable to shake the smile that pulled at her lips. Her fears remained but they prowled at a distance, kept at bay by her boyfriend who slept just feet away.

Chapter 3

Kate woke to the smell of waffles and thoughts of Reed. Stretching and smiling, she hurried into the living room but Reed's bed was empty. Then she spotted him in the kitchen. He wore Ember's **I will kill you if you touch my stove** apron, and was cooking waffles with Brittney and Ember.

"Good morning!" Reed said brightly. "Hungry?"

"Starved," she said.

She walked to him and leaned up to kiss him. "I like waking up to find you in the kitchen." She wiped stray flour off his cheek.

"Breakfast is almost ready," Brittney said.

"I love your waffles," Kate said.

"Oh these aren't Brittney's," Ember said. "These are Reed's."

"I didn't have everything here so I had to make do," Reed said.

On her way to the table Ember lowered her tone so only Kate would hear. "He refused to go to the store. Said that wasn't part of the date."

Kate's smile widened and she wrapped her arms around the chef. "I suspect it's going to be a beautiful day."

Marta yawned and entered the kitchen. "Why so early? It's not even eight yet—not that I'm complaining about the breakfast." She grabbed orange juice from the fridge and drank from the jug.

"Don't do that," Ember said, swatting her with a towel. "We aren't savages."

"You do it more than I," Marta countered.

"Only when it's almost empty," Ember said.

They sat down to breakfast and Kate scooted closer to Reed, marveling at how easily he inserted himself into the meal. They talked and laughed until Reed glanced at his phone and frowned.

"We'd better get going," he said. "We have class."

"I don't have class until—oh." Kate grinned. "I forgot I'm going to yours."

She dressed quickly and he vacated the bathroom for her to brush her teeth. Kate skipped the shower but brushed her hair, and then did a touch of makeup before exiting. Reed was already tying his shoes.

"Your roommates have a pool going on how long it takes for us to get tired of each other."

"Oh?"

"My bet was the full two weeks," he said, flashing his easy smile. "If I'm right, I get ten from each of them."

"Then let's prove them wrong," she said.

"You can't tell her the bet," Marta protested from the kitchen where she was still eating. "That's cheating."

"I agree," Brittney said.

Reed grinned and stood, catching Kate's hand. "Ready?"

"Let's do it," she said.

They left and took her car, for obvious reliability concerns, and went to his class. She enjoyed the lecture more than she'd anticipated and then they sprinted to make it to her class. Throughout the day they rushed between classes, pausing only for a quick lunch before running off to another. True to Reed's word, they spent every minute together, and she couldn't recall ever being so happy.

Despite the proximity with Reed and the joy it inspired, a cloud hung over them, and several times he received texts from Aura. At first she was hesitant to speak about Aura, but when she voiced her concerns he didn't hold back, and they talked several times about their worries.

To talk about Aura felt good but also strange. Kate had rarely held back with Reed, but this was the first time it was hard to speak her heart. The effort required seemed to draw them closer together.

The conversation shifted to many other topics, one of which was new boundaries. It was her least favorite part of the day but she tried not to show it. She was more than ready to take their relationship further, but tried to respect Reed's desire to take it slow.

Their time bled into the evening and she relished every minute. Reluctant to abandon him even to her own room, she remained on the couch until well after midnight and they were both falling asleep to their second movie.

The next day was Saturday and they went shopping, picked up things from his apartment, and played a game of basketball with Jackson and Shelby. The blondes joined them, making the game chaotic and filled with shouting and laughter, especially when Ember kicked the ball across the court, where it clanged off the backboard and bounced into the street.

"GOOOOAAAAAAAAAL," Jackson called.

Saturday merged into Sunday, where they took a walk and a picnic before opting to go swimming at the school pool. Monday they dived back into classes and did homework in the evening.

The week passed in a blur of smiles, kisses, and pushing each other's feet off the couch as they both tried to study on their laptops. The proximity ratcheted up the intensity of any physical contact, the kisses growing heated and passionate, his hands caressing her back and waist, but never wandering lower or higher.

Reed's ability to keep his hands in check was at the same time gratifying and frustrating. He proved time and again that he respected the physical space between them, a respect that could only be admired. But there were several nights where she wished he let his passion overcome his caution. And each night he kissed her goodnight and retreated to the air mattress on the living room floor.

Unwilling to miss out on the festivities, Jackson and Shelby were frequent visitors at Kate's house, and the six of them crowded onto the couches for movies and games. Brittney had a rarely used Wii that saw a lot of action, with Shelby schooling all of them on Mario Kart while Brittney bested them in bowling. At the end of the game, Ember complained she was better at actual bowling, so they went to the local bowling alley to see if she was right.

"You beat me by one pin," Jackson complained.

"It's still a win," she insisted as she put away her ball.

"She's right, Jackson," Shelby said, and then her smile turned smug. "And I beat you too, remember?"

Jackson laughed sourly. "I want a rematch."

"Anytime," Shelby said sweetly, patting his chest.

Several times others joined the group, including Tanner, Ember's new boyfriend. The guy was on the chess team but looked like an underwear model, right down the flowing lock of blond hair. He was shy and quiet, and unfazed by Ember's outbursts.

Ten days into the marathon date the consistent lack of sleep caught up to all of them, and irritations mounted. It started when Marta tripped over Reed's shoes and spread like a disease, with the girls all making snippy comments.

Kate new it was only temporary but noticed Reed retreat to the living room to do more homework, even though she was pretty sure he was already done. Annoyed, Kate followed him and asked about it. She spoke softly, but her voice carried enough acid that he looked up.

He stared at her until heat rose into her cheeks but she couldn't back down. Then he carefully put his laptop aside and stood. Without a word he wrapped his arms around her and simply held her gaze.

"What are you doing?" she demanded.

"Hugging you."

"*Why?*" she ground the question out.

His smile was cautious. "Because it's hard for me to be upset when I look into your eyes. I'm hoping the same applies for you."

Her lips twitched in irritation but her annoyance withered beneath his bright blue eyes. She scowled, inexplicably attempting to hold onto the anger before it could dissipate, but he merely held her bound, a slight smile on his face.

"I hate you a little bit," she finally said.

His smile widened. "Does that mean you've let go of your irrational anger?"

"Irrational?"

He feigned panic. "Er, just anger. I meant just anger. Can we go back to staring into each other's eyes?"

She laughed sourly. "Do you ever get angry?"

"Once," he said. "When Harold Blackwell stole my pencil in the sixth grade."

"Seriously," she said. "Do you not get angry?"

"Of course I do," he replied. "But I think Jackson has rubbed off on me. He just thinks everything is so funny."

"He's irritating too," Ember muttered, walking toward the door.

"That's just because you're like his sister," Reed said with a laugh.

She opened her mouth to retort and leveled an accusing finger at Reed, but all at once tears filled her eyes and she left without a word. The confusion on Reed's expression matched Kate's until Brittney entered and joined them.

"I forgot you didn't know," Brittney said, reading their features.

"Know what?" Kate asked.

"Ember lost her brother when they were teenagers," she said. "Car accident. I think someone lost control on ice and skidded into her car."

"I'm sorry," Reed said. "I didn't know."

"She doesn't talk about it," Brittney said. "I don't think even Marta knows."

"Knows what?" Marta asked, striding to them. When Brittney shared the story again Marta grimaced. "That's terrible, but why did she start to cry? We've talked about brothers all the time. And she has a younger brother."

"I think Reed was a little too accurate," Brittney said. "Ember likes Jackson and Shelby a lot, and Ember conspired with them more than the rest of us on during the dating challenge."

"Should I . . ." Reed gestured towards the door.

"Probably not," the three of them said in unison, and then Kate said. "The only thing Ember hates more than arrogant guys is talking about her feelings." Reed nodded but his expression was reluctant, so she put a hand on his arm. "Seriously, just let it go."

The previous anger had dissipated and Kate and Reed got ready to leave, but Kate caught Reed glancing to the door, his expression thoughtful. She wondered again what it would take to make Reed angry.

Chapter 4

Kate almost forgot about Aura as the days blended together. They spoke of her, and Kate occasionally thought of Aura's impending arrival, but her focus remained on Reed.

She learned he didn't like to put toothpaste onto his brush, and preferred to suck it right from the tube. The strange choice drew no small amount of teasing from the other girls, but he merely shrugged.

"Don't you hate it when the toothpaste gets all stuck in the bottom of the brush?" he asked. "Besides, the brush lasts longer than the tube."

Kate snorted and shoed the others away so she could step into the bathroom. The rule about private time remained, but four girls and one bathroom made time difficult, so they'd agreed to brush at the same time. She glanced his way and smiled, feeling all the while like a couple that lived together. Then she noticed toothpaste dribbling down his chin.

"You faf somfin on fur fin."

He chuckled. "Fut?"

She spit and pointed to his chin. "You have something on your chin."

"So do you," he said.

They laughed in unison and finished getting ready for bed. The next day they went to the post office to send his rent check, and to the bank to deposit her check from a recent tutoring session. They talked finances and budgets, and went shopping for weekly groceries, forcing them to choose what they were going to eat and when.

She got a close up look at his money. She'd expected him to be good with budgeting and was not disappointed, and he got a close up view of her Amazon addiction. His laughter ended when she saw his bank statement, and noticed how much he spent on sweet potato chips.

"They're delicious," he said defensively.

"But so expensive!"

"Worth it!"

They dealt with the mundane and the momentous, like when he received the news that one of the internships was interested in him and wanted an interview. She shared in his dismay when he learned his car needed new brakes, and he commiserated with her when she got sick. He even made her soup.

She'd dated Jason for years, but grew closer to Reed in two weeks than she ever had to Jason. The simplicity of daily life, shared through the lens of a marathon date, cemented their relationship in a way that felt permanent. For a glorious moment she imagined their future unfold.

"I don't want this date to end," she complained on the final night.

"This has certainly been an unexpected date," he said.

"Sure we can't continue?"

"No repeats," he said.

"Why not?"

"You know why," he said.

She wanted to argue but she didn't. Their time together had also led to a pushing of physical boundaries. Their kisses had grown more passionate, and she'd sensed his resolve weakening. She *wanted* to push against his barriers, but she didn't want to be the reason they were broken.

"Fine," she said with a sigh. "What are we doing tonight?"

143

"You had your date with cars, I have mine."

His cryptic answer reminded her of their date when they'd driven go-karts. She'd thought she would have an advantage, but he'd surprised her with his skill. Now they were driving again? How? Where?

She pressed him for answers but he refused, his smile turning teasing. "You'll see when we get there."

They left Boulder behind and drove to Denver. Prior to Reed, she'd thought it a long commute, but after two weeks together the time seemed to pass in minutes, and before she knew it they were pulling into a packed stadium. Then she spotted the signs.

"A crash derby?"

"Have you ever done one?" he asked.

"Never," she said. "But I always wanted to."

"That's what your mother thought, but she wasn't sure."

She smiled, still surprised by the normalcy of her boyfriend talking to her mom. They were guided into a spot by flashlight wielding employees and then headed to the front of the stadium, joining the raucous crowd.

The stadium was large, the stands big enough for thousands. Nearly full, they swelled with people carrying nachos and hot dogs, large sodas and beer. Families came with kids and groups of teenagers, all talking excitingly about the upcoming carnage. Then she ascended the steps and the arena came into view.

Rows of cars were lined up side by side, parked on a floor of sand. Ramps curved into large jumps and a pair of huge monster trucks sat between them. Their chassis gleamed, their enormous tires black and clean, just waiting to be filled with mud.

"I've always wanted to see a monster truck rally," Reed said.

"I assumed you'd already been to one," she said.

"Almost," he said. "Once. But the girl got strep throat and couldn't make it. I gave the tickets to Jackson and Shelby. I think it was actually their first date."

"And they hit it off?"

"From the first day," he said with a laugh. "Although their relationship was a little rocky at first."

"How so?"

"Later," he said, pointing to the arena. "They're about to fire up the engines. I brought earplugs if you'd like them."

"Will I need them?" she asked.

Two men climbed into the monster trucks and waved, and then the engines turned on. The roar of the engines was followed by a roar from the crowd. The blue truck spun, the tires digging into the dirt and sending a spray of soil into the air. It accelerated around the arena like a roaring lion, the sound of its engine drowning out thousands of throats. Then the second truck kicked on and Kate winced at the sound.

"Earplugs?" she shouted.

He handed her a pair and she put them in, diminishing the shrieking engines to a dull roar. Most members of the crowd didn't seem to mind the noise and cheered the screaming engines. Another two monster trucks came out and the four prowled around the arena, and Kate screamed her approval.

An announcer ascended the steps to the small stage at the edge of the crowd and grabbed the microphone. His appearance sent the four monster trucks to the four corners of the arena where the drivers killed their engines. Then he welcomed the crowd, his voice echoing through the arena as he introduced the cars and their drivers.

"This is incredible!" Kate shouted, awed by the enormous cars and what they were about to do.

"Just wait!" Reed called back.

When the announcer got up the trucks revved their engines and the blue one rounded the arena. It charged the smallest jump. The noise of the crowd swelled with anticipation as it reached the ramp and went airborne, and then landed on the line of cars.

Glass shattered and metal crumpled as the giant tires tore into hoods and trunks, the monster trucks bouncing over the crushed cars. The crowd roared its approval as the truck reached the end of the cars and sped away.

The next followed, and then the third, each truck trampling the cars into the dirt, shattering and smashing the cars like they were toys. Witnessing the awesome carnage left Kate shocked and breathless.

One truck landed with a wheel off the cars and tilted sharply. The crowd gave a collective gasp as the truck careened to the side and bounced off another ramp before righting itself. Kate laughed in delight and relief and looked to Reed, who was equally as shocked.

The trucks smashed cars for half an hour and jumped off the big ramps, streaking through the air amid cheers and screams. Kate enjoyed everything about the event, the screams, the whine of overpowered engines, the crunch of steel, the smell of chips slathered in nacho cheese. Kate screamed herself hoarse.

When the trucks exited the arena, the announcer returned to his platform and announced an amateur crash derby would be the next event. Reed caught her hand as the announcer continued to talk and pulled her toward the steps, guiding her out of the stands.

"Want to get something to drink?"

She nodded and they made their way to the concessions. The line was just beginning to form during the break and he was third, allowing them to grab drinks quickly. But instead of returning to their seats he pulled her to the end of the arena.

"Let's go check out the cars they're using in the derby," he said.

Sipping their drinks, she and Reed threaded through the crowd to the end, where six cars were parked behind a gate to the arena. All were painted in garish colors and she spotted a Toyota with a giant unicorn on the driver's side door. Several drivers were being outfitted with protective gear and helmets. One of the employees spotted Reed and Kate on the fence and walked over.

"You must be Reed and Kate," he said. "You ready?"

"For what?" Kate asked.

"We aren't here to watch," Reed said, a smile on his face. "We're here to *drive*."

Chapter 5

"How did you do this?" she demanded as they were ushered behind the gate. "One of Marta's cousins?"

"Nope," he said. "I bought plain old tickets. Saw it was coming to town and it sounded like fun."

"You bought the tickets months ago," she realized.

"Before our date on July 4th," he admitted. "I saw that it was going to be on the same day as a challenge date and couldn't resist. Plus I got a deal."

"Even at a discount these must have been expensive," she said.

"I thought it a nice investment," he said, his fingers threading into hers.

They were led to a man outfitting the others with helmets. As they joined the group, they were given a safety speech. It sounded like the exact opposite of everything she'd learned in high school. Hit the other cars but try not to hit the drivers. The doors were reinforced to protect them but a hard enough hit could break bones. Protect the engine and try to hit with the trunks. Don't do the jumps unless they wanted to die.

"We don't have to do this if you're worried," he said.

"Are you kidding?" she said. "I can't wait to crash into you."

"I think you did that eight months ago," he said with a laugh.

Excitement and worry seeped into her chest and escaped in a giggle. She leaned up to kiss him and then pulled her helmet on and strode to the car with the unicorn on the door. She ducked past the bars welded onto the roof and then shut the door, but it was already dented and it took two tries to get it to shut. A woman appeared in the window.

"Don't worry about the car none," she said. "After they're wrecked they'll be fed to the big trucks."

"Thanks," she said.

Kate grabbed the steering wheel and examined the interior of the car, which was about as trashed as she expected. The passenger seat was missing and the remains of the back seat were a dingy mess of brown cloth and torn leather. Dirt and bare wires were visible, the bones left from the stripped vehicle. Just trash waiting to happen. But not yet. It still had a final ride, and she was the driver.

A slow smile spread on her face as she turned the key in the ignition, the car coughing to life. All around her the other cars turned on and she looked to Reed. Sitting in the green Honda next to her car, he smiled as their eyes met.

"Ready?" he called.

"No!" she laughed.

The woman from earlier stood at the front of the cars and told them to spread out around the exterior of the arena, and when the announcer called for them to start, they were free to rumble. The other drivers revved their engines. A woman in the car next to Kate's fidgeted nervously as they waited, and Kate realized she was doing the same.

An employee pressed a button to raise the gate and the driver of the first car stomped on the accelerator, sending his car bouncing into the arena. He turned into a donut on the dirt, his white car kicking dirt all the way into the stands. They cheered him on but the woman shouted for him to get out of the way.

"What do we do if we're the only ones left?" Reed asked.

"We see who wins!" she shouted, eliciting a grin.

The other cars accelerated away and Kate went next, entering the arena amid a roar of cheers. Her heart soared as she drove to a corner, overwhelmed with the size of the ruts in the dirt. From up in the stands they'd been large, but on the ground they were enormous, and the car bounced over the giant troughs left by the monster trucks. She squeaked in surprise when her helmet struck the bar on the ceiling.

She took a breath to steady herself and then drove to the nearest corner. She backed into the corner and tried to steady her hands as she watched the others take their places. She swallowed and checked her mirrors, and laughed at herself for the habit. Then she put the car into gear and readied herself to crash into other cars, and the car driven by her boyfriend. She'd never felt so nervous and excited.

"Let's go!" she shouted, voicing the emotions roiling in her chest.

The announcer named each of them, and she took the time to lean out and wave when her name was called. Filled with adrenaline, she felt like she could sprint a mile. The horn blared and she flinched, and then stomped on the accelerator. Her car leapt forward and she struggled to keep on track, aiming for the nearest car. They'd said that if they used the engine to ram other cars their car would probably die first, but she didn't trust herself to drive backwards.

Four of the six cars converged on the center, while two hung back, clearly hoping to wait for the herd to thin. On impulse she swerved away from the larger collision and spun around one of the jumps. Her car bounced on the worn shocks and she slammed into the seat belt, but spotted the car coming around the other side of the jump.

The man's expression registered surprise and he tried to swerve, but hit a rut and spun. She braced for the impact and yanked on the steering wheel, sending her trunk into his car like a baseball bat. Her rear door on the opposite side smashed into the front of his car and bits of metal went flying.

She heard high laughter and abruptly realized it had come from her lips. She pressed on the gas and surged forward while the other driver tried to escape. But the impact had damaged his wheel and a grinding of metal came from his front tire. Seeing the opportunity, she braked and shifted to reverse. Then she stomped on the gas pedal, sending her trunk into the front of his car.

She slammed into the seatbelt as the impact rattled her bones and then looked over her shoulder. The other car was already trying to retreat and her blow sent it into the wall, where steam rose from the engine. Obviously furious at the quick exit, the driver shouted and hit the wheel.

" . . . would have thought the unicorn would be such a shark?" the announcer roared, and Kate suddenly heard the upswell of noise.

The sound was deafening, a cacophony of screams, shouts, and stomping of feet. Was someone singing? Or was it music? The roar was punctuated by the rending of metal and the snapping of plastic as another car crashed into the back of Reed's Honda.

A wide grin spread across her features and she tightened her grip on the steering wheel. Then she stomped on the gas pedal and streaked across the arena, hunting. The battle had pushed to the other end of the arena, out of view from her and her previous victim. Dirt splattered the wall, kicked up by her tires as she careened around the smashed cars. She bounced her way toward the three remaining cars smashing into each other like brawlers in a bar. The fourth had collided into the row of crushed cars and looked much like them except for the steam rising from the engine.

Kate spotted Reed, still in the game but trying to extricate himself from between the other two cars. The green Honda was a mess. Its trunk was open, its doors bent, and the front corner was misshapen. She vacillated between striking him or another, but then a woman aimed for Reed. Anger surged within Kate and she turned toward her.

Going as fast as the slippery dirt allowed, she streaked across the arena and smashed into the front of the woman's car just before she hit Reed, the impact sending her spinning away. It also sent Kate into the driver's side of Reed's car.

He rocked away from her and then stared at her, so she raised her hands helplessly. "Sorry!" she shouted.

She then laughed and put it into reverse to back up—but the other car slammed into Reed, knocking her to the side as well. She yanked on the steering wheel and tried to escape, but the impact had damaged the other driver's engine and he began to swear as his car rolled into a rut and didn't move.

Kate gestured to the woman's car and Reed nodded, and together they accelerated toward the remaining opponent. They all struck head on, and the woman's car died, rolling backward to bounce off the side of a ramp. The collision had sent Reed off course and around the ramp. Kate gained a devilish smile and pressed down the gas, sending her car after him. He saw her coming and swerved. The damaged front of her car slammed into his trunk, sending them both spinning.

Steam rose from her car, indicating the radiator had been cracked. Realizing she didn't have much time, she tried to retreat and accelerate again but Reed shifted to reverse and followed her to the wall, smashing her like a mosquito. Her car promptly died, leaving Reed the victor.

Chapter 6

The announcer called for them to exit the vehicles and she tried her door, but it was jammed. The opposite door bulged inward and she had no desire to climb into the back seat, so she opted to exit via the absent window.

"The unicorn takes a surprising second place!" the announcer called, his voice reverberating over the cheers. "But the Honda dragon wins the round!"

She stumbled out of the car, abruptly feeling the bruises from the impact. But her smile would not be constrained and she removed her helmet to see Reed approaching. His easy smile feigned worry and she slapped his shoulder.

"Couldn't let me win, could you," she said.

"I thought you didn't like that."

"I don't," she said. She wrapped her arms around his neck and leaned up to kiss him.

Workers entered the arena and helped the other drivers out of their cars, and then all six of them walked across the torn ground to the gate. They exited to find six more cars sitting ready with their drivers putting on helmets.

"What'd you think?" he asked.

"Painful, exhilarating, terrifying—and *awesome*," she said.

"They almost had me after you disappeared," he said. "Then you came charging in and sent that woman's car flying."

She grinned, reliving the memory and feeling the bruising impact anew. They continued to talk about the derby as they returned to their seats to watch the second batch of drivers, who now had to avoid the cars from the first. Kate cringed when her car took a hard hit and then cheered for more damage.

When they finished, twelve dead cars lay scattered around the arena and the monster trucks made a roaring return, crushing them to the delight of the crowd. After that they put on the final show, with all four racing, jumping, and crushing the cars in the arena.

When the dust and broken glass had finally settled, the crowd reluctantly filed out of the arena. Kate and Reed worked their way to the car and sat waiting for the line to move another inch. She sighed in contentment.

"That was epic," she said.

"You have dirt on your face."

"So do you," she retorted. Then she realized the derby was the end of their marathon date and her smile faded. "I can hardly believe the last two weeks was all one giant date."

"I don't think I've ever enjoyed a date so much," he said.

She looked at the trees lining the parking lot, their leaves well into fall, with some drifting down to land on the cars waiting to exit. She'd always loved the changing of the seasons but with each passing day she sensed a shift approaching, and she felt the approach of winter.

"Ready for Aura to come?" he asked.

"You know what? I think I am," she said. "You were right that spending time together would help. I find that I've grown sick of you."

He collected her hand and flashed the smile she'd grown to love. "I'm tired of watching you eat a bowl of cereal. You just chew so *loud*."

She fought the laugh and shook her head. "Not nearly as bad as when I saw you shave in just a towel. I mean, all those abs are just disgusting."

He coughed, struggling to keep his amusement from showing. "At least I won't have to see you in your sexy pajamas."

She smiled sweetly. "I put those on just for you."

He could hold it no longer and began to laugh. "I *knew* it."

"You and your shaving in a towel," she said, laughing as well. "It really wasn't nice."

"That's my normal routine," he protested. "I can't very well get shaving cream all over my shirt."

"True," she allowed, and then abruptly the amusement faded. "I'm going to miss you."

"I'm not going anywhere," he said. "I live five minutes from your house."

"I know," she said, looking out the window. The line had moved several cars and they were nearing the exit, and the end of their marathon date. "I'm just going to miss seeing you each morning."

"We're both behind on homework," he said.

"I know," she said. "Doesn't mean I have to like it."

"Don't worry," he said. "It's my last semester. Then we'll see what happens."

She threw him a look but his attention was on the cars as he pulled onto the street. The surge of hope was sharp, and she noticed a twitch to his lips, as if he'd meant what he said but also regretted voicing it. She settled into her seat, a small smile on her face. The seasons might change, but as long as she was with Reed, she would be fine, even through winter.

On the drive back to Boulder they relived the derby and the monster trucks, and reminisced about the last two weeks. When they finally reached her house, he dropped her off on the doorstep and kissed her goodnight. He'd already packed up his things and his bag sat in his trunk. She couldn't resist a final kiss and then slipped inside.

Her roommates were enjoying strawberries and whipped cream as they watched a movie, and Kate grabbed a bowl and joined them, wincing as she sat down. They wanted answers and she shared the events of the evening. They'd already known what Reed intended and wanted every detail. When she fell silent Brittney sighed.

"The last two weeks were fun for *me*—and I'm not even dating him."

"Me too," Marta said. "Can't we keep him?"

"Not now," Kate said. "We're both behind on our classes and Reed needs to finish his thesis." Privately she added, *and we need space to cool off.*

"I'm going to miss him," Ember said.

"Really?" Kate asked.

Ember nodded without taking her eyes from the screen. "I really like him," she said. "So I hope he doesn't break your heart, because I don't want to have to break his legs."

Kate smiled. "Thanks, Ember."

Kate gingerly leaned against the couch, grateful for the last two weeks, for Reed, for her roommates—even grateful for Aura who'd helped create Reed. She was as ready as she could be for her to appear, because somewhere in the last two weeks she'd realized the truth.

She was in love with Reed.

Volume 18: The Four Dates Date

Chapter 1

Reed took a bite of the apple, methodically chewing. He wasn't supposed to meet Kate until dinner but he didn't want to wait, so he left his car in the lot and walked to the engineering building.

Aura's family had arrived in Boulder a few hours ago, her latest text message weighing on his phone like a brick in his pocket. The last time he had seen her, she'd been withering away in a hospital bed. Now she would be on his doorstep after dinner.

He took another bite and checked his phone as he entered the building, the interior warmth a welcome reprieve from the freezing temperatures of early winter. Four hours to go. He grimaced and realized he'd checked the clock so many times his battery was going to be dead. He stuffed it into his pocket and ascended the stairwell to the third floor.

The corridor was empty so he took a seat on the bench outside Kate's classroom. Posters of engines and machines adorned the walls, while a notice board was situated across from him, its surface covered with flyers and papers. He noticed one inviting students to join Tau Beta Pi, the honor society for engineering students, and wondered if Kate had joined the program.

He would have preferred to join her class, but he knew she was taking a quiz. During their marathon date the professors had been very accepting, except when it came to quizzes or exams. He sighed and took another bite of his apple, his thoughts shifting to Aura.

It had been four weeks since he'd learned she was awake. He'd claimed the marathon date was for Kate's benefit, but it was also for his, and the proximity to her kept him from thinking of Aura. But now the day had come, and he could avoid it no longer.

His thoughts pulled to when he'd said goodbye to Aura in the hospital in Florida. It seemed like decades ago but it was just a couple of months. He'd waited three years and, just as he moved on, Aura was returning to his life. It felt like she'd risen from the grave. His feelings for Kate hadn't changed, but the love he'd had for Aura hadn't entirely disappeared.

He leaned his head against the wall and sighed, wondering what he could possibly do. What would he feel when he saw her? They'd spoken a few times over the last few weeks but she'd been brief, as if reluctant to speak over the phone. Hearing her voice struck a chord in his soul that thrilled him. And terrified him.

His phone buzzed and he pulled it out. To his surprise it was Kate. The text message was simple, and asked if he could meet her outside her class. He smiled and texted back a picture of him sitting on the bench, the image tilted to show the exterior of her classroom door. The reply came quickly.

Reach under your seat.

He frowned but did as requested, and knelt down to search under the bench. Then he noticed an envelope taped under the bench containing a single key and a list of directions. His confusion turned into a smile as he realized Kate had planned an invitation.

I thought we agreed we were skipping our challenge date today.

She replied with a smiley face. He laughed, the sound echoing down the empty hall, and then followed the first of the directions. It didn't have a destination or a map, so he had no idea where it was going to lead.

He reached the end of the hall and it directed him down the stairs and outside. Autumn now gripped Colorado and the trees on campus were glorious shades of copper, coffee, and fire. Leaves littered the ground and a freezing wind carried them away.

The directions told him to turn and follow the edge of the engineering building to the corner, and from there they pointed back into the engineering building. He frowned and reviewed where he'd gone, but it clearly said to enter the nearest door.

He swung the side door open and entered a stairwell that led upwards. He ascended several flights to the top of the building and then down a corridor to a grey door. The instructions indicated he should open it.

The sign on the door said maintenance and it proved to be locked. Producing the key, Reed looked both ways before unlocking the door and entering. The room beyond was large and filled with an assortment of tools and equipment. Large pipes ran along the ceiling and a boiler made the room stuffy and warm.

He flicked the lights on and followed the directions around the machinery to the back corner of the room, to an alcove and a ladder. Intrigued, he ascended the ladder to a small room on the roof. Then stepped into the open.

Taller than most of the buildings on campus, the roof of the engineering building provided an unbroken view of the university and the city, the lights of which were just coming to life. The sun was setting and vivid colors stretched across the horizon. Warmed by the machinery on the roof, the breeze blew across his shoulders, ruffling his coat.

He rotated to view the other side and found a table. Complete with two chairs and a white cloth, the table contained bread, salad, pasta, and two pieces of chocolate cake. He strode to the table and examined the meal.

"You're early."

He turned to find Kate picking her way across the roof. Dressed in jeans, a button-up shirt, and a jacket, she was stunning, her brown hair hanging over one shoulder. He smiled and stepped into the embrace.

"I thought we agreed no big date tonight," he said.

"You planned a marathon date," she said, her eyes sparkling. "I planned a miniature one. And did you really think I was going to let you spend time with Aura without a final reminder of me?"

"I suppose not," he said. "However did you book the table?"

"I made a new friend," she said. "One of guys in my class works in the building. He asked if he could help and I told him I wanted to take you to the roof. He loaned me a key."

He sat down with her and they began the salad course. Throughout the meal he caught her watching him, measuring his reaction. He saw worry in her eyes. At first he thought it was for herself, that she was worried about him choosing to be with Aura. But by the main course he wondered if it was for him, because she understood what he was going through and knew she could not help.

"You sure you don't want me to come with you tonight?" was the closest she came to talking about Aura.

"No," he said. "I think this is something I need to do on my own."

She nodded as if the answer was expected and steered the conversation to their plans for next week. He guessed she was avoiding the topic of Aura for his benefit and was grateful. Just being with Kate melted his fears and left him unfettered. But this close to seeing Aura, thoughts of her continued to surface.

"Reed . . ."

Realizing he'd stopped paying attention, Reed straightened. "I'm sorry."

"Don't be," she said. "I don't think I would know what to feel either."

"Is that what I'm doing?"

"Do you still love her?"

The question was blunt but said softly, as if she feared the blow it would land. She held his gaze as she waited, but he could see the budding emotions beneath her stillness. Reed wanted to assure her but didn't know how, so he told her the truth.

"I don't know," he said. "Her return has brought everything back up."

Kate looked away and then back. "I know."

"You know?" he asked.

"Love doesn't just evaporate because a person leaves," Kate said. "Remember Jason? I loved him for a year even after I broke things off. Talking to Aura will you give you the chance to let those feelings go."

I hope.

She didn't say it, but that's what he heard. She was gambling everything, their relationship, their future, their fate, all on him deciding he didn't love Aura. Although Reed wanted to argue with the risk, he couldn't, so he reached out and took her hand.

They finished the cake as the sun set. The miniature date was quickly cleaned up and they retreated into the building with a box of supplies. Reed cast a final look at the last light on the horizon before following her down the ladder.

Once they were out of the building they faced each other and she set the box down to give him a crushing hug. He felt the weight of the contact, as if she never wanted to let go, and hugged her just as fiercely.

"I'll see you when you're done," she said.

I hope.

He heard it again, and his heart ached. He gave her a quick kiss, and before he lost this nerve, turned and walked away. He knew if he looked back, he would find her standing alone on the sidewalk.

Chapter 2

Reed stepped into the hotel and came to a halt, torn between proceeding or walking out. The lobby was clean, the patterned carpet just a touch faded from the foot traffic, the wallpaper a neutral blue. Empty trays sat on the counter, the lights dimmed over the waffle station that seemed to have infiltrated all continental breakfasts.

Dressed in black and white, the woman at the counter looked up and smiled. "Checking in?"

"Just visiting a friend," Reed said.

The woman's eyes flicked to the lobby and Reed turned, spotting a girl rising from a chair. His breath caught as the figure from his past stepped into the light, the memories bursting across him in a swell of regret.

"Reed," she said with a slight smile.

"Hello, Aura."

She walked to him, her gait slow and measured, as if she was in pain. Tall and slender, she was nearly his height. Her blonde hair had been curled and reflected the light, enhancing the blue of her eyes.

Dressed in jeans and a white shirt, she looked just as beautiful as he remembered, right down to the slight smile, the one she'd always reserved for him. He walked to her and hugged her gently, like he would a sick child. The contact was warm and laced with memory, bringing a smile to his lips, and tears to his eyes.

"I'm not going to break," she said.

"I don't want to hurt you," he said, retreating.

"You won't," she said. "I couldn't move very well when I woke up, but I've been doing physical therapy every day and it's better now."

"You look great," he said.

She smiled tentatively. "Being asleep for three years does wonders for one's skin." Her eyes flicked to the woman at the counter.

Reed glanced over his shoulder to see the woman watching them curiously. "Do you want to go?" he asked, motioning to the door.

"Yes," she said.

"Where are your parents?" he asked, glancing about as if he'd missed them.

"Upstairs," she said, a flicker of irritation marring her flawless features. "They haven't left my side in a month, but I insisted I get some time alone with you."

He motioned toward the door. "Can you blame them? They thought you were dead."

"I love them," she said, a frown creasing her features. "But it's starting to get a little stifling."

For a moment they were quiet as they walked to his car. When they reached the decrepit Camry she ran her hand across the hood like it was an old dog. Noticing the affectionate look, he chuckled wryly.

"You never liked my car."

"I do now," she said. "And it's good to know some things haven't changed."

"Three years is a long time," he said.

"Not so long for me," she said quietly.

"I'm sorry," he said hastily. "I didn't mean—"

"Don't," she said. "You have nothing to apologize for. If it weren't for you, I wouldn't be here."

Tears abruptly filled her eyes and she looked away. Not knowing what to say, he opened her door and motioned inside. "We have plenty of time to talk."

"Are you sure Kate doesn't mind?" she asked.

They stood so close that he could see deep into her eyes, and they betrayed a vulnerability he'd never seen before. Not trusting himself to speak, he nodded his head and she smiled before slipping into the car. Then he walked around to the driver's side, taking his time in the hopes it would clear his mind.

At her request he drove her to the mall, and from there they walked through the nearly empty corridors. She paused often, asking questions about movie posters and electronics, all of which were new to her.

"I never thought about how much you missed," he said, watching her examine a new iPhone.

"Three and a half years," Aura murmured. "Everything feels different."

"Is this the first time you've been out since you woke up?"

She nodded. "I still have to think about walking, and it's like my legs don't remember how. My parents didn't want me to fall and get hurt."

"I can't believe you are walking at all," he said.

She flashed a faint smile and touched his arm. "I had a good reason to."

Stunned to silence, he watched her walk to a bank of iPads and marvel at their settings. When she tired of the electronics they left and continued to wander around the mall. They stopped by the bookstore and she bombarded him with questions about new releases and new books.

"You've missed a lot of good movies," he said.

"Like what?"

He tried to recall some and started with the Marvel movies, before talking about the Star Trek reboot and a handful of others. She listened in rapt attention, soaking in everything she'd missed like a starving man would a Christmas feast.

They visited a clothing store next and she browsed for tops. "I'm skinnier than I was," she said. "It's weird to wake up and find out that none of your clothes fit."

"I don't think a three-year coma is the preferred weight loss method," he said.

She smiled and shook her head. "Certainly not the top choice."

"What was it like finding out how long you'd been asleep?"

She paused in front of a rack of jeans. "You know those dreams when you go to class and suddenly realize you're naked?"

"Doesn't everyone?"

"It's like that," she said. "Except it's real. And it doesn't end."

He grimaced. "Sounds awful."

"They told me two days after I woke up."

"They waited two days?" he asked. "Why?"

"The doctors weren't sure if I was going to slip back into a coma, so they didn't want to cause me stress."

"So for two days you thought that the accident was recent?"

"It felt like a week had passed," she said.

Reed suddenly realized the weight behind her looks. To her, the accident had been just a month ago, meaning everything was still recent and vivid, undimmed by time. Their date—where he'd all but said he loved her—would be just a few months ago.

"So how do you feel about Tim?" he asked.

She laughed, the sound tinged with admiration and relief. "You know, everyone else has been so careful with what they say, like they're scared I'm going to go nuts. But you and I always had a relationship where we held nothing back."

"They're just worried about you," he said.

"I'm just tired of being treated like I'm made of glass," she said. "They're always changing the subject, always talking over me, never telling me the truth."

"Like about Tim?"

"He should have died in the accident," she said.

The unexpected vehemence in her voice caused several nearby to glance their way, their expressions uncertain. Aura didn't notice. Her features twisted in anger, she clenched and unclenched her hands.

"He took years of my life," she said, her voice soft yet dangerous. "And I'm just . . . *angry*."

"You aren't the only one," he said.

She raised an eyebrow at the sudden heat to his voice, and he realized his hands had turned into fists. He stepped away to examine a shirt but the anger roiled inside, threatening to burst. Its sheer power surprised him, but Aura didn't force the issue. After a few moments he sighed and turned back.

"Want to get some ice cream?"

He met her gaze, the anger in her blue eyes fading to amusement. "How do you do that?"

169

"Invite you for dessert?" He feigned puzzlement. "Like this. 'Want some ice cream?'"

She laughed and consented. They left the store behind and stopped in the ice cream shop next door. Once they had settled into a booth, she stirred the treat with a spoon and watched the colors melt off the plastic. She'd gotten a waffle cone but had already given it to him, a smile and a wink reminding him of the habit when they were in high school.

"Things taste different than I remember," she said.

"Like what?"

"I don't like bread as much," she said. "And spice isn't as spicy."

"You didn't get your favorite," he said, using his spoon to point to her choice, a raspberry sherbet.

"I don't know what my favorite is anymore."

They were silent for a moment and he studied her. She appeared relieved to be out and about, and content to merely explore with Reed, but he sensed a weight upon her that she wanted to share. He wanted to press her on it but was afraid to.

"How are things going with Kate?" she asked.

Taken aback, he said. "Good. Really good. How much do you know?"

"Quite a bit," she admitted. "My parents showed me Ember's blog in an attempt to keep me from coming."

"They tried to stop you?"

"They thought you were happy," she said. "And they didn't want me to mess things up for you. They've always liked you."

"Your dad didn't like me after the accident," he said.

She frowned, her forehead creasing in a touch of anger. "My mom told me what he said to you. You didn't deserve that."

"I thought I did," he said.

"You're dodging the question," she said. "How are things with Kate?"

"Tonight's taking the place of one of our challenge dates, actually."

She winced. "I'm sorry about that. I really wanted to see you and tonight was the only night I could be in Boulder."

"I see her every day, now," Reed said.

"When you arrived at the hotel I didn't think you'd changed. Now I can see you have. Is it all from Kate?"

He considered telling the truth, that he'd changed because of her accident. Then Kate had finished the job, helping him heal from a wound that had remained open since the moment he'd listened to Aura's deathly scream.

"And because of you," he finally admitted.

Chapter 3

"Me?" Aura asked, pausing in finishing her ice cream. "How so?"

He looked away and then back. "I felt like if our date had been better, you would have wanted to be with me. And you wouldn't have ended up in that car with Tim."

"That's ridiculous," she said with a snort. "You really thought you could have stopped my accident?"

"If our date had been the best of your life, would you have stayed with Tim?"

"Yes," she said, and then grimaced. "Probably. One date doesn't change things."

"The last three years says you're wrong," Reed said.

"What do you mean?"

"I promised I wouldn't let it happen to another girl," he said. "So I promised you I would plan five thousand dates for other girls, and show them the standard they should expect."

"You can't be serious," she said, staring at him. "Why five thousand?"

"One for every second I was on the phone . . . listening to you die."

She held his gaze, shock momentarily binding her tongue. "You did that because of me?" Her voice had softened.

He shrugged. "It sounds a little stupid when I say it out loud, but for three years it dominated my life. I went on three thousand dates and never even held a girl's hand."

"Until Kate," Aura said.

"Until Kate."

She stood and tossed her bowl into the trash. "Tell me about her?"

Aura's expression was conflicted, as if she didn't want the answer. But she repeated the request so, as they left the mall behind, Reed began with their first date. He continued to tell the story of their dates in the car, filling in the gaps that weren't on Ember's blog.

She asked him to take her to a place where they could see the city, so he drove her to one of the parks on the nearby mountains, where a recent snowfall hadn't melted. Covered in white, the slope stretched away to the twinkling lights of Boulder. Evergreen trees were covered in snow and ice, their green boughs dusted like the snow was powdered sugar.

He put the car in park and shifted in his seat. "Now you know the story."

"I'm glad to see you happy," she said, looking at her hands.

"Why did you want to come back?" he abruptly asked.

"You weren't always this bold," she said. "It's a good trait for you."

"You didn't answer the question."

The questions that had bubbled inside of him boiled to the surface and he didn't retreat. At first he'd been worried about asking too much, about hurting the girl he'd already hurt. But he could wait no longer.

"I don't know," Aura said. She didn't look at him. "I guess I hoped there was a chance for me to make things right."

"What do you mean?"

"Did you really listen to me die?" She finally looked at him.

He swallowed and looked out the window. The snow had just begun to drift down, a silent storm that muffled all sound, dampening the night and leaving them alone. He shook his head but the words would not be constrained.

"That's what it felt like."

"Can you tell me what happened?"

"They didn't tell you?"

She shook her head. "The doctors thought it might be traumatic. Will you tell me what happened?"

"If the doctors didn't . . ."

"Please?" she asked, reaching out to touch his arm.

He swallowed at the contact. It was light, but sent sparks up his arm and into his chest. He'd wanted her to touch him for so long, but the triumph was fleeting, quickly replaced by thoughts of Kate.

The snow continued to fall outside the car, forgotten as he looked into her eyes. He wanted to resist but there was a pleading about her expression that could not be denied, so he agreed with a nod.

"You called me because Tim wouldn't let you drive. You were afraid."

"I remember that part," she said. There was a desperate need in her voice, a need to understand what had happened to her.

He looked away. "I heard his voice in the background, him yelling at you to hang up the phone. Then I heard the impact . . . and the crunch of metal and steel. Your scream seemed to last forever."

She took his hand and held it, like she was comforting him. He swallowed as the tears came to his eyes and fought the rising emotion.

"And then?" she whispered.

"I used the house phone to call 911, but you had skidded off the road and they couldn't find you. So I just listened to your breathing and kept talking, hoping you would respond. But you just got quieter and quieter.

"They said your car flipped six times after it struck the guardrail, that your car looked like a crushed can of soda. Tim was thrown free and broke his leg while you ended up pinned inside the car."

She rubbed her chest. "I remember the weight of it pressing against me, of the roof against my head."

In halting words she described the accident from her perspective, of the fragments of memory she retained. She'd felt as though time had stopped and light had been extinguished, leaving her in darkness, near death.

"I don't remember much of the accident," she said. "But I remember pain . . . and I remember your voice."

"You remember my voice?" he asked.

"You told me someone was coming," she said, her eyes distant. "You told me you where there. It's the first time I ever heard you swear. You swore so much."

"You were dying," he said. "I was in agony."

"You kept me alive, Reed," she said, meeting his gaze. "You gave me hope that I would survive, that I would have a chance to walk again. Do you remember telling me that? That you would take me wherever I wanted? That you would take me to the beach and go hiking in the mountains. You refused to believe that I would die. As I listened to you talk I realized Tim was the one that took my life. You were the one to save it."

Reed struggled to speak but she shook her head and leaned closer to him, her gaze holding him fast. "There is one more thing I remember," she said. "You told me you loved me."

Reed finally managed to speak, his thoughts leaping to Kate. "I did. Then."

"Don't you see?" Aura asked as if he hadn't spoken. "You were right. We were friends for a lifetime and it took dying for me to see that we were destined for each other. That you would always protect me, always love me."

"Aura . . ."

He didn't love her. He'd felt it the moment he saw her at the hotel, felt it when she looked at him, when she smiled. When she touched his arm and hand. When he'd visited her hospital bed in July he'd said goodbye, and the only emotion that remained was friendship. Throughout the evening he'd sensed the vestiges of his love evaporating away like steam from a cooling fire.

He struggled with what to say, to help her know that their time had ended. Especially after what she'd endured, how could he crush her without leaving her broken? Mistaking his silence for consent, she closed the gap in a rush.

Caught by surprise, he froze for an interminable moment. Then his brain registered the impending kiss and he retreated, instinctively raising his hands to her shoulders so she could not follow.

"Aura," he said, "this isn't what you want."

"It is," she said, leaning forward again. This time he saw desperation in her eyes.

"I'm sorry," he said. "We did spend a lifetime together when we grew up, that life ended. What I feel for Kate . . ."

Stung, Aura retreated and folded her arms, her body going rigid. "I've heard enough about Kate."

"Aura," he pleaded, "you have to understand. For you it's been weeks. For me it's been years."

"So I mean nothing to you now?" she demanded. "Just like everyone else? I'm just someone from the past that . . ."

Her eyes filled with tears and abruptly she crumpled. Tears dripped down her cheeks and she wrapped her arms around her stomach, her hands clenched like they would hold her body together. Her body trembled as she sobbed.

"I've lost everything, Reed. My parents are different, my friends are gone. Even the house I grew up in is sold. Everyone I've ever cared about has moved on. There's nothing left. And now even you are saying it was another life."

He reached out and pulled her into a hug. At first she resisted, but then wrapped her arms around him, sobbing into his shoulder. He heard the pain in her cries, the fear and doubt that had plagued her for weeks. She'd probably put on a brave face for her parents and the doctors, but the helpless rage of what she'd lost had built within her, boiling until the pressure was set to explode. He wanted to speak, but merely held her as she wept for the life she had lost.

Chapter 4

Aura cried for a long time, and Reed didn't move. It felt like he was keeping her from shattering, like her body would just crumble to dust if he didn't hold her together. When it finally subsided she shifted and he retreated.

"I'm sorry," she said. She grabbed a napkin from the cup holder and wiped at her eyes.

"For what?" he asked. "Feeling lost?"

"I'm sorry for dumping all this on you," she said. "You don't deserve it."

"We're not in love," Reed said. "That doesn't mean we aren't friends."

She managed a sad smile. "Guys can't have friends that are girls— not when they have a girlfriend."

"Does it break the laws of physics?" he asked.

She released a bark of laughter. "No, but I suspect it would cause more conflict than you want."

"You're right," he said. "You and I can't be friends. But *we* can be."

She wiped her eyes of the lingering tears, her expression one of puzzlement. "What do you mean?"

"Do you have feelings for me?"

She regarded him for several long seconds and then slowly shook her head. "I think I wanted to. You did save my life, and I guess I wanted to hold onto you. Does that make you feel bad?"

"No," he said. "I'm relieved. But I hope we can be friends—and I mean real friends."

She cracked a smile. "Like we were before you started to like me?"

"Yes," he said.

"But how," she asked. "There's no way Kate is going to be okay with this." She grimaced. "And I did try to kiss you. I'm so sorry. I'm just floundering and wanted something to latch onto."

"I'll tell her," he said. "But if you become *our* friend . . ."

"You think that's possible?" she asked, a tremor of hope in her voice. "I really don't want to lose my only friend right now." Tears welled up again.

"Let's go," he said, reaching for the gearshift.

"Right now?"

"You only have tonight, right?"

She nodded. "What are you thinking?"

"I don't know," he said. "But we've got twenty minutes to come up with something."

On impulse he pulled out his phone and called Kate. She picked up on the first ring. "Reed? Is everything okay?"

"I think so," Reed said. "But we have a problem. We've decided that to remain friends, she has to be friends with you."

Reed held his breath as he listened to the silence on the other end of the line. He knew he was risking a lot by putting her on the spot, but it was his only chance at helping Aura. If Kate said no, he would have to say goodbye to Aura. Permanently. There was just too much history between them and, if it came to a choice, his heart was with Kate.

"If she's a friend of yours, she's a friend of mine," Kate said cautiously.

"Can I talk to her?" Aura asked.

"She wants to talk to you," Reed said.

Reed handed her the phone and then backed out of the parking lot. As he drove down the mountain Aura began to speak. Tears came to her eyes again, the emotion thickening her voice.

"Reed is a good guy, Kate. Since I woke up I've been lost, but he's helped me see that I will be okay. And I really would like to get to know you . . . if you'll let me."

Reed tried to quiet his breathing but Kate's response was inaudible. The next several minutes became a game of frustration as he listened to her sounds of agreement and brief answers. Aura even laughed once and glanced at Reed, a motion he found to be distinctly irritating. It wasn't until he was pulling into his driveway that she hung up.

"Kate's on her way."

"Really?" he asked. They got out and she walked around the car. "What else did she say?"

Before Aura could answer, Kate's car appeared at the end of the block and she drove up to the house, but instead of pulling into the driveway, she parked on the road and got out, leaving the engine running.

Reed stepped to Kate and embraced her, highly conscious of the fact that Aura was watching. When they parted Kate smiled and motioned to her car, which Aura was already walking to.

"What's going on?" Reed asked.

"You wanted us to be friends," Kate said so Aura couldn't hear. "This is me trying. We'll be back later."

"So what am I supposed to do?" he asked.

She pointed to his house. "Do what I did. Sit around and worry."

She flashed a faint smile and strode to her car, leaving him on the lawn. "This wasn't how I planned for tonight to go!" he shouted.

Kate merely waved and pulled out her phone. She typed a quick text and then put her phone away before pulling onto the road. Just as she disappeared, his phone buzzed with the message she'd sent.

I can't promise we can get along but I promise I'll try. Sometimes girls just can't be friends.

He sighed and sent a quick reply, grateful for her effort. Then he looked around himself, wondering what he was supposed to do now. It wasn't very late, so he shrugged and walked inside. To his disappointment, his house was empty.

He'd had weird dates before, but this was the first time he'd been abandoned halfway through the night. He sent a quick text to Jackson, who responded a moment later saying they'd gone bowling.

Reed stared at the empty house and then groaned. He sank onto the couch and stared at the TV. He had homework, but that didn't sound appealing. Neither did watching a movie by himself. Then Jackson sent another text.

Don't just sit there. Get over here.

He grunted in amusement and picked his keys up for the second time. Ten minutes later he was parking at the bowling alley. Once inside, he paid and collected shoes and a ball before joining Jackson and Shelby. The blondes were also present, as was Tanner, Ember's new boyfriend.

"Thanks for the invite," Reed said to Jackson, sitting to lace his shoes.

"Everyone crashes and burns," Jackson said sagely.

"I didn't crash and burn," he protested.

"Your date abandoned you for your girlfriend," Shelby said, her tone apologetic. "I'd say that's the pinnacle of crashing and burning."

He endured their laughter and finished lacing his shoes. It may have been a weird night, but at least bowling would keep his mind from dwelling on Kate and Aura. Besides, if he didn't hear anything it would mean they were getting along. Right?

Kate had apparently been bowling with the others when Reed had called. Reed took her place, continuing Kate's game where she'd left off. It made him smile to look up and see Kate's name on the screen and know the end score would come from them both.

"How are Tanner and Ember doing?" he asked Shelby, lowering his voice so only she would hear.

"Good," she replied. "He's shy, and I think he's intimidated by our group, but his quiet protects him from Ember's anger."

Jackson and Shelby were about to bowl, and he jumped forward to beat her in sending his ball down the lane. She scowled as his ball hit the pins first, but a smile took its place when she got a strike a moment later.

"Being first doesn't make you best," she said sweetly.

"I still have a higher score," he said.

"But you've got a split," she replied. "Good luck with that."

She laughed and strolled back to her seat. Ember went next, and managed a spare. When she returned, Tanner quietly congratulated her on the frame. Tall and very muscular, Tanner liked working out and playing football, but he was the quietest guy Reed had ever met. He was also one of the best chess players in the chess club.

Tanner raked his dark hair back and then adjusted his glasses before nodding to Reed. "Good to see you again," he said.

"You too, Tanner," he said. "How's your semester going?"

"Better," he said.

Tanner's eyes flicked to Ember and then he flushed. Noticing the interchange, Ember smiled and put her hand on his knee, causing him to flinch. Reed shook his head, wondering what had made him so shy. Jackson leaned over.

"Shelby and I have a bet going if Ember will make him run. You want in?"

"Ten bucks says they stay together through Christmas."

Shelby smothered a laugh as Jackson raised his eyebrow. "Really? Do you see how red his face his? He may be twice her size, but he's got the heart of a kitten."

"But he likes her a lot," Reed said.

Jackson shrugged. "It's your money."

Reed watched Tanner with Ember, his thoughts once again on Kate and Aura. He'd traded places with her like a wrestler tagging another into the match, and in a weird way, he'd never felt closer to Kate. She may have been with Aura, but Kate was still on his team.

Chapter 5

"Well tonight was a weird date," Jackson said to Reed as they left the bowling alley behind.

"You mean Reed and Kate swapping places?" Shelby asked. "Definitely weird."

"Do you want to talk about it?" Jackson asked.

"I'm fine," Reed said, checking his phone for the thousandth time.

"Are you *sure* you don't want to talk about it?" Jackson pressed.

Reed looked to his roommate to see his meaningful look, like he needed to talk to Reed privately without Shelby overhearing.

"Yeah," he said. "Shelby, do you mind?"

She glanced between them and then shrugged. "Call me later," she said, kissing Jackson before walking to her car.

Reed and Jackson got into the car and Jackson pounced. "This probably isn't the best time, but you promised to help me plan."

"Your engagement," Reed said with a groan. "I'm sorry. I've been so busy I haven't had a chance to figure it out with you."

"You're always with Kate," he said blithely. "I can't fault you for that, can I?"

Reed glanced at him as he pulled out of the parking lot. Jackson had a smile on his face but there was a tightness about the expression that revealed irritation. Reed grimaced as he realized that once again, he'd abandoned his friend.

"I'm sorry," Reed repeated. "With Aura and everything I—"

"It was *Aura*," Jackson said with a dismissive wave. "And you needed to deal with all that. I'd give you more time but Shelby's getting suspicious."

"How suspicious?" Reed asked.

"Very," Jackson said. "She's started to ask questions I can't really answer."

"We have fifteen minutes until we get home," Reed said. "You think we can plan how you're going to propose by the time we reach the driveway?"

"It'll help keep you distracted from thinking about Kate and Aura," he countered.

"Done," Reed said. "What do you want to do?"

"Something memorable," Jackson said, "but not fancy."

"That's not really your style," Reed agreed. "Do you know what you want to say?"

"Bits and pieces," he said. "But it's not like I have it all figured out."

They discussed ideas and discarded several. As they talked Reed resolved to focus on Jackson. Even before officially dating Kate, Jackson had taken nearly two weeks to take him to Florida, and after they got back they'd hardly spent any time together. During the marathon date Reed hadn't even been home.

He glanced at the clock and realized it had only been a half hour, and Kate was unlikely to be done anytime soon. Loath to sit around and worry, he decided that now was the best time to work things out with Jackson.

"Hey," Reed said. "Why don't we go play in the park and keep figuring out what to do. You think Shelby would mind?"

185

Jackson swept his hand to Reed. "Does the great Reed have time for little Jackson?"

"He's making time," Reed said. "And if he's great, it's because of his roommate."

"It's weird to hear you talk about yourself in the third person."

"You started it," Reed said.

Jackson laughed, the sound lacking the touch of worry from earlier in the conversation. He texted Shelby to let her know, and a few minutes later they stopped at home and changed into basketball clothes. Then they drove to the nearby park. A handful of people were playing on the illuminated courts but there was plenty of room, so Reed and Jackson chose an empty one.

"Only left hand?" Jackson asked.

"It still won't be fair," Reed said.

"You've got skill," Jackson said. "If you spent a little time practicing you'd be as good as me."

"Practicing won't give me six inches."

"I'm not six inches taller than you," Jackson protested.

"But you play like you are," Reed said, throwing him the ball.

Jackson smirked and shot from outside the arc, sinking it into the net with ease. Reed retrieved the ball and sent it back to him, but he sank it in again. Reed caught the ball and dribbled it outside.

"How do you do that?" he asked.

Jackson accepted the ball from him. "You have a gift for understanding women. I have a gift on the court. Ready to play?"

They started a game but Jackson's heart clearly wasn't in it, and Reed actually scored several points. Jackson didn't seem to care. He played only with his left hand but gave up several drives where he could have easily stopped Reed.

"What's on your mind?" Reed asked.

"I'm just wondering if I'm ready for marriage," Jackson said. "I'm not exactly the poster boy for commitment."

"Do you love Shelby?"

"Of course," he said.

"What about marriage scares you?"

"I don't know," he said. "You've been my roommate, so you know how messy I am."

"Shelby does too," Reed reminded him, trying to dribble to Jackson's left.

Jackson swiped the ball and took it outside before draining a three. "I just see you and Kate and worry I'm missing something."

Jackson had always been more open during games, his usual penchant for finding amusement in serious situations taking a temporary backseat to the pressures of the game. Reed was disappointed to realize they hadn't played since he'd met Kate.

"Every relationship is different," Reed said. "Are you having second thoughts?"

"I just wonder if I'm husband material," he said. "I'm in college and a year from graduation. Do I really want to tie myself down?"

Reed caught the rebound from a rare Jackson miss but remained in place. "I think you're looking at this the wrong way," he said. "Most guys can't find the right girl for years, but you get to enjoy college with her. Isn't that better?"

"Probably," Jackson said.

"Besides," Reed said. "If you found the perfect team, would you ever want to play with someone else?"

"No," Jackson said, a smile on his face.

"Then what are we talking about?" Reed asked, tossing him the ball. "Let's plan this engagement."

Jackson grinned and caught the ball. "I think we should use a basketball," he said, dribbling to the hoop.

"To propose?" Reed asked, incredulous.

"It would be perfect," Jackson said. "Just think. We are playing around, she doesn't know what's happening, and then I switch the balls and there's something inside. Then she finds the ring."

"Sounds perfect for you," Reed said with a smile. "But I'm not sure it's right for the girl."

"Maybe," he said. "But how would you do it?"

"Me?" Reed asked. "I'm light years from a proposal."

"Says the guy that's clearly in love."

"You think so?" Reed asked, snatching the ball from his hands and shooting. "What makes you say that?"

"The way you look at her," Jackson said. "And for a guy that clearly knows the mind of a woman, you've been rather dense about figuring it out."

"What are you saying?" Reed asked. The ball clanged off the rim and bounced into the grass, forgotten.

"Kate's in love with you," Jackson said.

"She can't be," Reed said, but his voice faded as he heard the truth.

Every look, every smile, the way her green eyes softened when she looked at him. The heat in his chest burned bright as he thought of Kate's lips pressed against his. He shook his head, afraid to speak it aloud.

But did he feel the same? The prospect terrified yet thrilled him, and he looked away from Jackson's triumphant smirk. But if Kate was in love with him, why hadn't she said anything? Why would she hold it back?

"She's waiting for you, Reed," Jackson said.

"You think she's waiting for me to say it first?"

"Do I have to solve everything?" Jackson asked, sweeping his hands wide. "You drive slower than my grandma—and she's in a walker. She's loved you for weeks—probably months—even if she didn't realize it herself. The blondes, Shelby, even Tanner knows it and he's just barely started hanging out with us."

"Tanner?" Reed asked.

"Yes, Tanner," Jackson said. "The guy asked me if you and Kate were engaged. He's hung out with us *twice*, and he knows it. Why can't you see it?"

"This doesn't feel like what I felt for Aura," he said.

"That's because you loved her like a teenager crush," he replied. "That's not what you feel for Kate. You have that undying—kiss forever—passionate and lasting kind of love that everyone wants."

"How can you possibly see all that?" Reed protested.

"Because that's what I feel for Shelby," he said.

Jackson began to laugh and put his hands on his hips, the sound echoing over the court. Nearby players stopped their game and pointed as Jackson's amusement washed over them. Then he thrust his hands in the air.

"I'm getting married!" he shouted.

"Congrats, bro!" someone shouted.

Jackson whooped and clapped Reed on the shoulder. "Good game, brother. I needed that."

As Jackson jogged to retrieve his ball, Reed remained in place, struck by the ramifications of what Jackson had suggested. Then he felt a thrill as he thought of Kate and looked to the sky in chagrin. He wasn't ready to shout it to the heavens, but he found himself wondering.

Was he in love?

Chapter 6

They walked to the car and went home, arriving just minutes before Aura and Kate returned to the house. Shelby had waited for Jackson, so Jackson clapped Reed on the back and left him on the porch. Reed waited for the girls to approach.

"How was your time together?" Reed asked, walking up to Kate and Aura.

"Good," Kate said. "I enjoyed hearing stories of you as a kid."

"And I enjoyed hearing stories of Reed as an adult," Aura said.

"Friends?" Reed asked.

Aura looked between them and slowly shook her head. "I think it's time I figure out my life."

"Is that a no?" Reed asked.

"It's a not right now," Aura said. "Tonight I've realized I'm okay. Someday I hope to have friends like yours."

"So you're going?" Kate asked.

"My mom and dad are on their way to pick me up," Aura said. "I just wanted to say goodbye."

Kate hugged her first. "It was nice to meet you," she said.

"You too," Aura said. "Reed deserves someone great."

"I think that's a bit much," Kate said.

Aura merely smiled and stepped to Reed, who embraced her. Reed didn't know what the girls had talked about, but it seemed to have helped Aura. She looked worlds better than she had when she'd been crying in his car.

"It was good to see you," Reed said when they parted.

"You too, Reed," she said. "Make sure you take care of Kate for me."

"I'll do that," he said.

A rental car pulled up and Aura's parents got out. While her father fussed over her, Sheila walked to Reed and hugged him, clinging to him with surprising strength. When she stepped back her eyes were filled with tears.

"Thank you, Reed—and Kate," Sheila said. "I know tonight was probably hard, but she needed it."

"Sheila!" Harold called. "We need to get her back. The doctors said she needs a full night's sleep."

"Goodbye, Reed," Aura called.

Reed waved, struck by the strange sense of finality, as if it was the last time he would see her. Aura smiled one last time and then she was gone. As the car disappeared around the corner he released a long sigh.

"Weirdest date of my life," he said fervently.

"Agreed," Kate said. "Just goes to show, if you aren't dating me, it's going to be terrible."

He laughed and pulled her into his arms. "I'm glad I ended the night with you."

"Are you sure?" Kate asked. "Aura told me she tried to kiss you."

He winced. "I was going to tell you about that."

She wrapped her arms around his neck. "Oh? What would you say?"

"That a non-ex-girlfriend was in a bad place and briefly thought I was her salvation."

"And you stopped her?"

"Of course," he said.

She gave him a searching look and then smiled. "At least your fourth date will be with me."

"Fourth?" he asked.

"First was with me. Second was Aura. Third was with Jackson."

"He kept his hands to himself," Reed said defensively.

"At least one of them did," she said with a laugh.

"And what did you mean, fourth? It's after eleven and it's been a long night."

"I couldn't let anyone else have you at the end of the night," she said. She smiled mischievously and kissed him. "Come on. It's more of a double date with Jackson and Shelby."

He cast a look to where Aura had disappeared and nodded, grateful the night was over. Then he walked with Kate into the house. Inside, they found Jackson and Shelby pulling out every box of cereal in the house and putting them on the table.

"What's going on?" Reed asked.

"You don't drink but Kate said you needed one," Shelby said. "So tonight we're doing cereal shots."

Reed laughed and took a seat, accepting the shot glass from Jackson. "I'll take a shot of Lucky Charms," he said.

"Coming right up," Jackson said, pouring a tiny amount into the glass.

Reed drained it and savored the marshmallows. Kate asked for the same, a double, while Shelby took a glass of Cinnamon Toast Crunch. Jackson took Golden Grahams, but the box was mostly crumbs, so he stared at the nearly empty glass morosely.

"What a night," he said.

"Aura tried to kiss Reed," Kate said.

"Really?" Reed asked Kate as they stared at him. "Did you have to tell them that part?"

Kate suppressed a smile. "Can't a girl torment her boyfriend a little?"

"She almost kissed you?" Shelby asked.

Reed nodded. "To her, the accident was just two months ago, and she remembered my voice keeping her alive. Add that to the shock of learning how much time had passed and she latched onto me. She thought I was the only thing left."

"She just needed to heal," Kate said.

"By kissing Reed?" Jackson asked, smiling broadly.

"Are we done laughing at my expense?" Reed asked.

"Not even close," Jackson said with a devilish laugh.

Reed washed away his chagrin with a double shot of Fruity Pebbles, and chased it down with a shot of milk from a second glass. Shelby kindly topped him off and he nodded his gratitude.

"First time I've had four dates in one night," Reed said.

"Enough about you," Jackson said. "I want to know about Kate's time with Aura. That had to have been weird."

"It was at first," Kate said, examining her glass. "But she's more lost than anyone I've ever met."

"I can't imagine what that would feel like," Shelby said. "Just waking up and finding out years have gone by."

"Might as well be a decade," Jackson said, swallowing a glass of Captain Crunch like it was whiskey.

Reed laughed at the absurdity of the moment. "Is it just me, or is dating a minefield?"

"Of course it is," Jackson said. "Whatever made you think it wasn't?"

Shelby leaned over and kissed Jackson. "There are still mines after you've been dating, you know."

"What's that supposed to mean?" he protested.

"You know what it means," she said.

Jackson looked to Reed and gave a helpless shrug but his eyes were pleading. Taking the hint, Reed raised his glass.

"I think a toast is in order."

"We don't have any bread for toast," Jackson said, causing Kate to groan and hit him.

"To finding the right one," Reed said.

They toasted the end of a strange night and talked until after midnight. Then Reed walked Kate to her car. He caught her hand as she reached for the handle and pulled her back. He threaded his hands around her back and pulled her in tight.

"Tonight was interesting," he said.

"Can we *please* do a real date next time?" she asked.

"I already have a plan," he said.

"It's my turn," she complained.

"It should be," he said. "But I have a good reason. Jackson asked for my help and I need yours."

"What's going on?"

Reed told her about Jackson and his plan to propose to Shelby. When he finished Kate had a strange smile on her face, as if she'd known it was coming.

"Shelby knows it's coming," Reed guessed.

"She suspects," Kate said. "But that doesn't mean we can't have a little fun."

"Exactly," he said. "That's why I think our next date isn't about us. We get to set up some things for Shelby."

"So we're on the same team?" she asked. "I like the sound of that."

Reed nodded, a slow smile spreading on his face. "Let's plan an engagement."

She agreed, but Reed's thoughts returned to the realization he'd had on the basketball court. The girl in his arms was more than just a friend, more than a companion, even more than a girlfriend. And as they talked about Jackson's proposal he realized the truth.

He was in love with Kate.

Volume 19: The Ring Date

Chapter 1

Kate watched the clock on the wall, counting the seconds until she could get out of class. She'd wanted to skip class to help set up, but Reed had insisted she go. To her dismay the professor didn't seem to notice the hour, and a full minute passed before he glanced at the clock.

"Is class over already?" he asked himself and then frowned. "I suppose I can finish next time. Don't forget we have a quiz on Friday!"

By the time he finished speaking Kate was at the door and the first into the hall. There she found Reed waiting. He grinned and they hurried to the stairs together, rushing down and outside.

The weather had turned unseasonably warm, melting the first snow of winter and briefly returning the city to autumn. Students had flocked to the grass, taking advantage of the warmth and sun. Reed and Kate rushed through the Frisbee throwers and the girls sunning themselves to reach the parking lot. Three minutes after leaving the classroom, they were driving away.

"What's still left to do?" Kate asked, looking at the sky to gauge the time. "It's already getting dark."

"I already picked everything up," he said. "Are you ready?"

"Ready," she said, a thrill seeping into her gut. They'd planned dates for each other, but this was the first time they were planning one together. Granted it was for Jackson's girlfriend, but it was fun being on the same side.

"I'll make sure to act surprised," she said.

"You won't need to act," he said, his easy smile appearing on his face.

"What's that supposed to mean?" she asked. "I thought tonight was for Shelby."

"It is," he said. "But you didn't really think I'd leave you with nothing, did you?"

She laughed, the sound tinged with admiration and excitement. After Aura's visit, Reed had been even more attentive, and she frequently noticed a strange glint in his eyes, like she was an object to be admired and studied. Rather than feeling disconcerting, it left her wondering what had changed.

"Where's Shelby?" she asked.

"On her way to your house," Reed said. "Jackson just texted to let me know."

They drove to Kate's house and he dropped her off. Reed caught her hand and leaned into a quick kiss, the contact a promise of more. He grinned and waved to Shelby's car, which had appeared at the end of the street.

"Don't give it away by being too excited."

"I won't," she said, and then giggled. "I'll try not to."

She strode to her door as he got back into his car. Reed backed out of the driveway, vacating the space for Shelby, and waved as he drove away. Even though Kate knew she would see him soon, she waited on the porch until he disappeared, and then opened the door.

She hurried inside and ditched her backpack and jacket before the doorbell rang. Ostensibly there for a girl's night, the participants, except for Shelby, had an ulterior motive. Marta swung open the door and Shelby entered with a sack of chips and dip for the night.

"I wasn't sure what to bring," Shelby said.

"Brittney usually handles our edibles," Ember said. "But any contributions are welcome."

Brittney poked her head into view from the kitchen. "Get comfortable."

Shelby removed her shoes and sat on the couch. "This may come as a surprise to you," she said, "but I haven't been to many girls' nights."

Kate picked a bowl of dip and a handful of chips and sank into a seat. "Why not?"

"I always had my teammates," she said. "But it was always about the game. There wasn't much time to just hang out."

"What about on the off season?" Ember asked.

"There was no off season for me," she said. "I played basketball in the fall, soccer and softball in the spring, and a lacrosse league in the summer."

"I didn't know you played lacrosse," Ember said, and motioned to the house. "I started playing it when there was a guy on the team I wanted to date."

"Really?" Shelby asked. "We should play sometime."

"Another day," Brittney said, entering and placing a tray of fruit, dip, chips, and cheeses on the ottoman. "Tonight we're binging Halloween movies."

"Because Halloween is next week?" Shelby asked as she examined the tray with interest.

"Of course," Kate explained. "But we trade off. Last month was fantasy movies. The month before that was thriller."

"This is more organized than I'd anticipated," Shelby said.

"Girls' night is serious business," Ember said, claiming her favorite seat at the corner of the couch. "It's our only chance to avoid men so we can talk about them freely."

"Is that what we're doing tonight?" Shelby asked, her eyes sparkling as she picked up a chip.

"Of course," Kate said.

Kate watched Shelby settle into the evening. At first she seemed stiff and uncertain, the confusion hidden beneath a smile. But Kate had seen the way she sat at Reed's and Jackson's house and knew when she was relaxed.

Over the last several months they had all become group friends, with Reed and Jackson merging with Kate and her roommates into one large group. As Jackson's girlfriend, Shelby was furthest from Kate and Reed, the epicenter that had brought them together. She'd rarely spent time with just Kate and the blondes. As the minutes passed, Shelby gradually settled in and even contributed to the argument of whether Twilight was considered a Halloween movie or a romance.

"There are vampires," Marta insisted, "and sort of werewolves. That makes it Halloween."

"Vampires that sparkle," Ember said. "That makes it romance."

"Is it bad if I say I haven't seen the movies?" Shelby asked. They all looked to her and she shrugged. "I never really got the chance to. Are they good?"

Ember snorted and pointed to the rack of movies set next to the TV. "I'm changing my stance for tonight only. It's Halloween."

They all laughed and Kate stood to put the movie in, giving herself an excuse to look at the clock on the stove. She'd checked her phone so often Ember had given her a warning look, but Kate couldn't resist. She could almost feel the doorbell about to ring.

To her dismay her gut was wrong, and they were twenty minutes into the movie when the doorbell did ring. Sitting closest, Marta stood and opened the door to reveal a massive box sitting on the porch. Confused, Kate leaned over and stared at the box.

"What's that?" she asked.

"I'm guessing it's another Reed invitation," Marta said, eyeing the box that was as large as their refrigerator.

When they were all on their feet, Kate looked to Shelby. "Do you know anything about this?"

"Nothing," Shelby said, raising her hands. "But it's big enough for Jackson to hide in. What do you suppose it is?"

"Let's get it inside," Ember said.

They had to work together to get the heavy box inside, but it caught on the threshold. Kate cried out as her hands slipped and the others jumped free, allowing the box to slam into the floor. They all stared at the fallen box.

"I hope he wasn't inside," Shelby said, making them all laugh.

They got a pair of scissors and began opening the box. As they worked, Kate found herself on the receiving end of many looks and she tried to surreptitiously shake her head, feigning ignorance. When they finally got the heavily taped box open they found a second, albeit smaller, box inside.

Ember groaned. "I hope it's not a thousand boxes going down to a tiny little piece of cardboard."

An hour later they stood in a massive pile of cardboard, tape, and packaging paper. It covered the couch and stretched into the bedrooms and halfway up the stairs, the sheer volume of cardboard causing Marta to shake her head.

"It looks like Reed robbed a FedEx store."

"More than one," Shelby said, her eyes lit with delight.

Kate realized it was the first time Shelby was involved in the opening of an invitation, but she managed to hide the smile that threatened to blossom on her face. Brittney swam through the sea of cardboard to the kitchen and returned with her camera.

"Ready," she said.

Kate held up the tiny box that had been at the center of the enormous package and carefully undid the bow. Then she cut the tape with the scissors and unfolded the top of the cardboard. Inside, she found a carefully folded note.

She read it and then shook her head. "This isn't right," she said.

"What's not right?" Ember asked.

"The invitation isn't for me," Kate said, and turned to Shelby. "It's for you."

Chapter 2

Shelby stared at Kate in surprise. "What do you mean, it's for me?"

"It has your name on it," Kate said.

She managed to keep her smile contained as she passed the note to Shelby, who stared at it in astonishment. Then a slow smile spread on her face, suffusing her expression with delight. She looked to each of them.

"Jackson did this?"

"It certainly wasn't Reed," Kate said.

"But I don't understand," she said. "It says I'm supposed to go to the Eleven without a Seven, where Seven Ate Nine."

"I'd suggest you start with streets," Ember said.

"Ember," Marta said in exasperation. "He wanted her to figure it out on her own."

"Are you all in on this?" Shelby asked, skewering them with a look.

"Guilty," Brittney said, but her expression was unapologetic.

Confusion and excitement washed across Shelby's face and then she examined the note anew, a small smile flickering on her face before she registered disappointment. She swept her hand at the room.

"But what about girls' night?"

"Another time," Kate said. "We promise."

Ember grunted in amusement. "Most girls' nights we complain about the guys *not* doing enough. You actually get to do something."

Shelby nodded and shoved the note into her pocket before collecting her purse and striding to the door. Kate noticed she took long strides, like she was trying to control her excitement and not quite succeeding.

"I'll see you after?" Shelby asked, pausing in the doorway.

"Maybe," Marta said with a smile. "Now go follow the clues."

Shelby laughed nervously and nodded before departing. When the door shut Kate nodded to the girls and they scattered. Two minutes later they all re-entered the living room dressed in black. Ember even had black face paint on her cheeks, the pattern making her look like a diminutive commando.

"That's not going to help you hide your hair," Marta said with a smile.

"That's what this is for," Ember said, donning a black beanie.

"I've always wanted to be a ninja," Brittney said with a giggle.

Kate grinned. "You know what to do. I'll see you when it's done."

With excitement pumping through her veins, Kate stepped outside and sprinted down the block to where Reed's car idled. Also garbed in black, he grinned as she dropped into the passenger seat.

"You look good," he said.

"So do you," she said. "But why did it take so long to get the box onto our doorstep?"

"The box snagged in Jackson's truck and we had to do an on-the-fly repair job."

Kate recalled extra tape holding the outer box together and realized it had been there to keep the box from falling apart. As Reed pulled onto the street Kate gestured to the clock, which showed after eight.

"We're behind schedule."

"Jackson has it figured out," Reed said.

"You aren't helping him?"

Reed shook his head. "I helped him come up with the clues, but it's been mostly him."

"It was fun seeing Shelby so excited after the invitation," Kate said. "It reminded me of when you dropped off the cauldron of skittles for me."

He flashed his easy smile. "I was actually worried you would eat some before realizing they had letters on them."

"We've come a long way since then," Kate said.

"Further than I thought," he replied. She raised an eyebrow and he backpedaled. "I never imagined I'd get such an incredible girlfriend out of the challenge."

"Nice save."

"I try."

She laughed and pointed to the back of the car. "Is the ammunition ready?"

"I finished it while you were in class."

She smiled in anticipation. "Is it bad that I'm excited to do this to her?"

"Were you excited to hose me down with water guns?"

She laughed at the memory. "Enormously."

"I think she's going to love tonight," he said, and then his smile turned sly. "And so will you."

She wondered what he had up his sleeve but in that moment didn't care. They pulled into the park where they'd had their very first date and parked. Then they went to the trunk and each picked up a container filled with water balloons. She felt the urge to giggle as they hurried out onto the field.

Lights filled the park and the grassy expanse beneath the hill, while a corner of the hill lay shrouded in darkness behind a grove of trees. Withdrawing two water balloon launchers from his backpack, he handed one to her and they hurried to string them up between the trees. Just as they finished, Jackson appeared and raced onto the field to deposit a box at the base of the slope.

"You ready?" he called up to them.

Kate grinned and loaded a water balloon. She aimed for him and released, sending the balloon over his shoulder to splatter against the ground. Reed laughed and Jackson joined in, his amusement rolling up to them.

"I'll take that as a yes," he called.

He turned and raced back to his car, driving away to leave the park vacant for Shelby, who was probably just finishing the stop that Ember and Brittney were charge of. Kate fidgeted in the tense silence, her apprehension mounting . . .

—A water balloon exploded against her side, sending water across her body. She flinched in shock and turned to see Reed looking around as if in confusion. But he couldn't stop the smile.

"Where did that come from?" he asked.

"Same place as this," she said, sending one at him.

He ducked, but she grabbed another one and sent it into his chest. Reed stood, sputtering, as water dripped down his face. As he tried to wipe it off his neck she grabbed another balloon, bracing herself for retaliation.

"She's here," Reed said, pointing over her shoulder.

"I'm not falling for that," she said.

He smothered a laugh. "I'm not saying I wouldn't use the distraction tactic, but not this time."

He stepped to his launcher and loaded the balloon, the action finally convincing her he wasn't trying to get her to turn around. She looked to the parking lot and saw Shelby's car pull into a stop. She got out and looked around before spotting the box sitting in the vacant field.

Shelby slowed as she advanced onto the grass and paused. She peered about before withdrawing the clue and reading it again, obviously trying to parcel out the meaning. Kate hadn't seen the finished product, but an earlier draft had warned of the minefield she would have to brave to get the third clue.

Kate looked to Reed and found him armed and loaded. He nodded to her and she took aim, grateful they'd spent time practicing a few days ago. Then she released, sending the water balloon soaring into the night.

In the darkness and patches of light from streetlights, the small water balloon was impossible to see. Kate's balloon barely missed Shelby and exploded right behind her, sending water against the back of her legs. Reed's fell short, splashing her shins. Shelby gasped and retreated, searching for where the balloons had come from.

"When she figures it out, she's going to run," Reed whispered.

Kate was already loading another. "Then keep firing," she said.

They loaded and fired as quickly as they could, raining balloons down on the bewildered Shelby. Then she surged into a sprint, dodging and swerving to make herself harder to hit. Kate smiled as she recalled Jackson taking the role of target in their practice session, enduring many hits as he prepared his troops.

Reed hit Shelby's arm while Kate's balloon hit her leg. Shelby didn't slow. Graceful and athletic, the girl danced across the field even better than Jackson, and Kate felt a touch of envy for the girl's athleticism.

Bombarded by water balloons, Shelby skidded to a halt and picked up the box, but Jackson had added weights to the message. She cursed as she picked it up and raced back, but slowed by the box, she was struck several times, the water balloons drenching her as she escaped the battlefield.

When she was out of range Shelby put the box down and put her hands on her knees, panting. The smile on her face was evident even in the darkness and distance, and Kate realized that Shelby had enjoyed the war enormously.

"I can't believe she had fun," Kate said as Shelby loaded the box into her trunk. Shelby paused and read the new note within the box while she dried herself with the towel that had also been present.

"Jackson and Shelby have always been competitive," he said. "They enjoy a challenge as much as the victory, so Jackson's invitation is designed to test her."

"I would have hated this," Kate said.

"I know," Reed said. She heard the smile in his voice and turned to find him with a water balloon in each hand. "You'd rather face your opponent," he said.

"True," she said.

In a surge of motion she snatched a water balloon and hurled it, and the darkened hilltop dissolved into laughter and water balloons, the furious battle lasting until he tackled her and broke a water balloon on her stomach.

"Got you," he said.

She smiled and leaned up to kiss him. "Yeah you do," she murmured.

Chapter 3

When the balloons were gone they reluctantly cleaned up the mess and returned to the car. They squished their way down the slope, their shoes leaking water at every step. Then she slipped. She squeaked in surprise and caught his arm, but his wet shoes slipped as well, causing them both to tumble down the hill.

She laughed as she rolled to a stop. "I'm blaming you for that."

"Why me?" he protested.

"Because you started throwing balloons at me," she said.

He stood and helped her up. "I'll take *half* the blame," he said.

"Then I get half the credit," she said smugly.

He laughed and wrapped his arms around her back. "You know, I don't think I ever thanked you for starting the dating challenge."

"You're right," she said smugly. "That's one thing that I get *all* the credit for."

"I can't argue with that," he said.

"That's the first lesson a boyfriend needs to learn," she said. "That the girl is always right."

He reached up and caressed her cheek, moving a wet hair out of her eyes. "You're a good teacher."

He leaned down and kissed her. Soft and tender, the contact sent desire pooling in her belly. She forgot the chill from the water and the discomfort of her wet clothing, the box leaning against her leg, even the breeze on her wet skin. Her hands snaked up and held his neck, threaded into his hair while she clung to the warmth he inspired.

When they finally parted she gazed into his blue eyes. "What was that for?" she murmured.

"There's something I want to tell you," he said, his voice quiet, inviting.

"What's that?" she asked.

A spark of fear threaded into her chest. It was not the fear of loss or worry, the openness to his expression did not suggest that, rather the stillness before a memorable moment. She realized she was holding her breath.

"Kate," he said. "I . . ."

His phone rang, startling them both and shattering the moment like glass. He held her gaze for a moment as his phone rang and then kissed her briefly. A smile played across his features.

"Sometimes I hate phones," he said.

"Me too," she said, her heart thumping against her ribs. She had to swallow to clear her throat. "It's probably Jackson. Our job isn't done yet."

"To be continued," he said.

"I look forward to it."

He picked up his phone and she listened to Jackson ask how it went. Reed answered normally but remained inches from her, his other arm still around her back. His eyes never left hers.

"We'll be there in a few," he said. "We have to stop and change first."

"Hurry up," Jackson asked. "Or you're going to miss it."

"Shelby wasn't the only casualty from the water balloons," Reed said with a smile.

"Well stop playing around and get back here," Jackson said with a laugh.

"We're on our way," he said. He hung up and put his phone into his pocket, still looking to Kate. "We'd better get going."

"Today is about Jackson and Shelby," she agreed.

He smiled and nodded. "We come later."

Another thrill took her breath. "Let's go," she said.

She reluctantly retreated and felt the cold for the first time. Shivering, she hurried to the car and they left the park behind. The heat in his car had decided to quit again so they shivered all the way back to her house, where he dropped her off.

She rushed inside and stripped. Leaving her wet clothes on the bathroom floor, she turned on the shower and then laid out her dress for the evening. She'd forsaken her usual green for a red and black number, the red a series of artistic curves and whirls that gradually gave way to the black hem.

Her phone rang and she saw it was Reed, but instead of a voice call it was Facetime. She glanced down at her naked body and then grinned. Tipping the camera up to just show her face, she answered.

"What's with the video call?" she asked.

"I'm almost done," he said. "I thought you'd like to talk while we finished getting ready."

The screen showed him in a black button up shirt with a red tie that matched her dress—even though he hadn't seen it. She shook her head, realizing one of her roommates had told him what she intended on wearing.

"I'll be over to pick you up in a minute," he said.

"I think I'll meet you there," Kate said. "I decided to take a shower so I'm running late."

"A shower?" he asked. He looked up from where he was tying his shoes, and Kate tilted the camera to reveal her bare shoulders.

His eyes widened and he spoke in a strangled voice. "Okay, I'll meet you there!"

She laughed and flipped her hair. "You sure? You could come over if you'd like . . ."

"No," he said, and then grunted in chagrin. "Do you enjoy tormenting me?"

She gave a devilish laugh and tilted the phone back to her face. "Yes," she said. She blew a kiss. "I'll see you soon."

He shook his head. "Don't be late."

She hung up and left the phone on the desk. Taking a fast shower, she quickly dressed and tied her hair back. Then she donned her black heels and lifted the dress so she could hurry to the car. On the way, she picked up the sleek black mask that contrasted with the green in her eyes.

A glance at the clock in her car revealed her tardiness and she grimaced. She drove to campus as fast as she dared and parked at the arena where the basketball team played their games. Instead of a sports night, the parking lot was full of couples, all dressed up for the Fall Masquerade.

As she hurried inside she passed men and women in formal attire, and she smiled in anticipation of seeing Reed. Music throbbed from inside and she threaded her way through the crowd until she reached the arena floor. Then she slowed to a halt, her eyes lifting to the ceiling.

The basketball court had been transformed into a medieval courtyard. Pillars lined the exterior with cloth draped between them, closing off the view of the seats. Greenery had been added to make the floor resemble a courtyard, while lights glowed in the canopy.

Packed with dancing couples, the floor vibrated with the music. The annual dance was a tradition on campus and always occurred the Friday before Halloween. Kate had always wanted to go but Jason didn't like to dance, and so she'd sat home and discovered an affinity for Cinderella.

She walked up the tunnel, advancing past walls of cloth rippling in the air to reach the dance floor. Spinning images of masks and jewels swirled across the ceiling and walls, while the jumbotron had been covered in mirrors, reflecting the lights in a dazzling display across the arena.

A slow dance replaced the fast song and dancers paired off, turning beneath the dim lights. She picked her way through the dancers until she spotted Reed, who stood at center court with Jackson. As if sensing her approach, he turned, and her breath caught.

She'd never seen him dressed up, and in the dark suit he looked stunning. He stood with one hand in his pocket, leaning to the side like he'd just emerged from a magazine. His blue eyes lit with admiration at seeing her and traveled up and down her form.

She closed the gap and looked up into his eyes. "You look amazing," she said.

"Not compared to you," he said, and leaned down to kiss her.

"You're late," Jackson said, "but you look stunning."

"Thank you," she said. "When's Shelby supposed to be here?"

He looked at his phone. "A few minutes."

Kate noticed his nervousness and stepped close. "She loves you," she said. "She's going to say yes."

"We'll find out soon enough," he said, releasing a nervous breath.

He stepped out of view and pulled a stand into place on center court. A basketball sat atop the stand and Jackson pulled out a small box from his pocket. He balanced it on top of the ball and nodded to them.

"I'm ready," he said.

Reed reached for Kate's hand and led her through the dancers to the table at the side of the arena were several employees were running the lights and music. One of them spotted Reed's approach and stood.

"Is Jackson ready?"

"I think so," Reed said.

"We've got their song all cued up," he said. "Just say the word and we'll hit the music and the spotlights."

"What's he going to say?" Kate asked, craning to look at the tunnel where Shelby would emerge.

"I don't know," Reed replied. "He wouldn't tell me how he wanted to propose."

Kate's phone buzzed and she pulled out her phone. "Marta says she's here."

Reed caught Jackson's eye and waved. Jackson straightened his suit and then stepped into the crowd just out of view of the stand. Those around the circle noticed the ring box on the basketball and began to whisper to each other, the speculation spreading like wildfire.

Kate looked to Reed and found him watching her, his eyes lit with excitement. He smiled and leaned down to kiss her, softly. Her stomach flipped from the contact and then she looked to the tunnel just as Shelby walked into view. Reed spotted her as well and motioned to the DJ, who faded the music.

At the sudden absence of the music, students shifted uncertainly until a spotlight appeared and descended on Shelby. Other spotlights appeared, shining in a line between her and center court. By unspoken accord the crowd parted, leaving an aisle to the basketball and ring box. It also allowed Kate to get a good look.

On the stop Marta had been in charge of, Shelby had found the dress and the mask, and she looked stunning in black and white, the two-toned dress highlighting her blond hair. Her mask was ethereal, revealing her beauty.

"Jackson?" Shelby called, her voice uncertain.

There was no answer, and she uncertainly advanced down the aisle of light to the ball at the end. She slowed as she saw the velvet box and didn't notice Jackson appear behind her, reaching her side just as she picked up the black velvet case. Her breath caught as she carefully eased it open. The light glittered off the diamond ring.

"Shelby," Jackson said.

She turned to find Jackson down on one knee, and her hands flew to her mouth. Jackson merely smiled as if he wanted to savor the moment, and tears came to Shelby's eyes, a strangled sound of joy escaping her lips.

"I never want there to be a day that you aren't on my team," Jackson said, his voice filling the silent arena. "And I promise that if you join me, I'll let you be the captain." She laughed through her tears and he grinned. "Shelby Sewell, will you marry me . . .?"

Chapter 4

Shelby held the diamond ring in one hand, her other hand in Jackson's grasp. Tears were in her eyes and her throat worked, but no words came out. Jackson merely waited, his lips betraying a hint of a smug smile, as if he knew he'd done good.

"It's about time," Shelby finally said.

"Is that a yes?" Jackson asked.

"Of *course* it's a yes," Shelby said.

The smile finally broke free and Jackson stood. Wrapping his arms around his newly minted fiancé, he spun Shelby about as they kissed. The students who had gone silent at her entry now cheered, whistling and stomping their feet to voice their approval.

The DJ leaned over and turned a dial, amping the sound until the speakers boomed the song, *Highway to Hell*. Kate snorted and looked to Reed, but he shrugged and gestured to Jackson and Shelby.

"Apparently it's their song," he said.

"Of course it is," Ember said, her voice incredulous.

Jackson finally put Shelby down. Unable to contain it any longer, Kate led Reed, Ember, and Brittney across the gap to embrace Shelby. Flushed with excitement, she hugged them all and let them admire the ring, which was large enough to spark a touch of envy in Kate's chest.

"It's beautiful," Kate said.

"I thought tonight was just an invite to a date," Shelby said, swatting Jackson. "And what was with the water balloons?"

"That was us," Kate admitted.

"We were the other racers on the track," Brittney said, motioning to Ember.

"And I did the lasers at the third location," Marta said, stepping into view, now dressed in a beautiful red dress.

"You certainly made me run a gauntlet to get here," Shelby said, her words exasperated.

"I couldn't let you get here without a sense of victory," he said, his smile turning smug.

"Is that what marrying you is going to be like? Victory?"

"Of course it is," he said. "But like I said, you get to be captain."

Kate grinned as she watched them kiss again, but her eyes drifted to Reed. He watched his roommate with an expression of deep satisfaction, and she recalled that Shelby had met Jackson because she'd gone on a date with Reed. Then Shelby rounded on Reed and Kate.

"I must be the only girl *ever* that had to brave water balloons to get an engagement ring."

Reed laughed wryly and swept his hand to Jackson. "He made us practice on him until we could aim better."

Kate watched Shelby as she looked between her friends and Jackson, the excitement evident in her eyes. She'd known her for only a few months and had frequently been impressed by her caliber.

When the initial euphoria of the proposal faded they joined the dance in earnest. When a slow song came on Reed asked her to dance, and whisked her into their own space. Surrounded by people, she only had eyes for Reed.

"I've never seen Jackson so happy," he said.

"Shelby looks pretty happy too," Kate said, glancing at the newly engaged couple. Shelby was admiring the ring, showing it off to a few girls who had approached.

"Has all this reminded you of Jason's proposal?"

She met his gaze and cocked her head to the side. "You know, it hasn't. You've made me forget all about him."

She said it in a teasing tone, but the truth to the words surprised her. Even with all the planning, she'd never once thought of Jason's failed proposal, and she marveled that Reed had made her forget one of the most painful memories of her life.

She draped her hands on his neck and looked into his eyes. Partially hidden behind the dark mask, his smile was soft, the tenderness extending into his eyes. He brushed a finger across her cheek, eliciting a tremble.

"You make me happy too, you know," he said.

"I hope so," she said. "Because I can't imagine a life without you."

Because I love you.

The words were on her lips, aching to be voiced. But a burst of fear kept them in check. He leaned down and kissed her, and she sought to convey what she felt with her lips. As the music picked up she continued to turn a slow circle, trapped in his embrace.

When they parted his eyes revealed a hint of excitement. "Can I show you something?"

"Of course," she said.

Reed caught her hand and led her to Jackson. Pulling him aside, he spoke in an undertone away from Shelby and the others. Curious, Kate tried to eavesdrop, but by the time she closed the gap Jackson was nodding.

"We'll see you when you're done," he said.

Reed nodded. "It shouldn't be more than an hour."

"What won't take more than an hour?" Kate asked.

"We have a stop to make on the way home," Reed said, leading her from the dance floor.

"At this hour?" she asked. His gait was hurried and she picked up on the thread of excitement. "It's nearly ten."

"I know it's late," he said. "But it won't be there tomorrow and I'd really like you to see it."

Leaving the arena behind, they got into his car and he pulled out of the driveway, turning in the opposite direction of the road leading to his house. Before she could ply him for answers, he asked a question of his own.

"Have you ever been involved in a proposal?" he asked, removing his mask. She did the same.

"My first," she said. "You?"

"Second," he said, "but I don't think I can count the first one. I was six, and my uncle made me stand in a little suit holding the ring."

She imagined a tiny Reed holding a ring, his hair combed perfectly, his suit pressed and neat. But at six he'd probably been fidgeting and annoyed at what he was being asked to do. She wondered if he'd dropped the ring.

"Jackson's proposal was beautiful," Kate said. "Right down to the choice in song."

"Everyone's story is unique," he said. "But it still surprises me how there's no correlation between why two people fall for each other."

"You're doing the psychology thing again."

"Sorry," he said with a self-deprecating laugh.

"People just fall in love," she said.

"That makes it sound like it's an accident," he replied. "Like it's a star that's just waiting to strike them on the skull and suddenly they're in love."

"Isn't that how it happens?"

"I think that's how attraction happens," he replied. "But I think love is a choice."

"How so?" she asked.

"Attraction gives a push," he said, "but it's our choices afterward that will determine if that attraction deepens to love."

"So that's what happened with Jackson and Shelby?"

"Jackson liked her and decided to ask her out. Then they decided to play on the same team, a choice that led to a number of fights and a breakup."

"You did say their early relationship was rocky," she said, recalling a comment he'd made at the crash derby. "But I didn't know they broke up."

"They were broken up for two weeks," he said. "Then he saw her in a pickup game and they ended up on the same team again, only this time the game was just two-on-two. They each kept hogging the ball and ended in a fight about it. Turned out they both wanted to impress the other, and their fight ended in an embarrassingly passionate kiss."

"I take it you were watching?"

He grinned and nodded. "They lost the game, but they've been playing together ever since."

"Now I understand the captain comment," Kate said.

"Exactly," he said. "And their choices then led to now."

"What's this all about?" she asked with a teasing smile. "Are you trying to say something?"

"Maybe," he said.

Her heart fluttered as conversation took a sharp turn. His blue eyes glimmered with emotion, his easy smile on his lips, but it was not an expression of amusement. She swallowed as he took her hand.

"Would you mind clarifying that statement?" she asked.

"In a moment," he said. "We're almost there."

She scowled. "I don't think I like this teasing."

"Sorry," he said, and she could see he meant it. "This is just something I really want you to see."

"And it will be gone tomorrow?"

"It happens once a year," he said. "But I actually missed it the last few years."

"So you've done it before?"

He grimaced. "I know I promised you I wouldn't take you on a date where I'd taken another girl, but this is something you don't want to miss."

"What was her name?"

"Kendra, I think," he said. "She was nice and liked the outdoors, so I took her to the pile."

"The pile?"

"That's what I call it. I'm actually surprised no one else had done it, but I guess if they had, the city would have taken measures to stop it. It does make a little bit of a mess."

"You've really piqued my curiosity," she said.

"I'm hoping it's there," he said. "I wanted to drive by and check but I never got the chance the last couple of days."

"Is this Reed Hansen admitting he didn't plan a date?" She feigned shock.

He laughed and pulled into a parking lot behind one of the government buildings near city hall. "I hope this makes up for it," he said.

She squinted into the grounds of the building. Trees dotted the area but lights from the building and parking lot illuminated the grass. Many of the trees showed the fall wear, their branches a patchwork of remaining leaves.

He pulled off the road into a parking lot, where he exited and came around to open her door. When they got out he led her around the corner of the building into a field lit by towering lights. During the day it was the grounds of the government building.

She came to a halt when she saw their destination. A massive mound of leaves. Raked to the center of the park, the pile had likely been gathered from throughout the grounds. The leaf pile was at least ten feet high and as wide as a house.

She shook her head in disbelief. "I've never seen one so big."

He smiled at her surprise. "Every year they gather every leaf around the building into a single pile. For one night only, the pile sits until the trucks come to haul it away."

"Are we going to . . ."

He gestured for her to go first, his expression one of delighted anticipation. "Care to jump in a leaf pile?"

Chapter 5

"I'm in a dress," she said.

"And I'm in a suit," he replied, removing the jacket—a motion that momentarily distracted her.

The adult in her wanted to shake her head and argue, but the kid would not be restrained. She giggled and put her purse down, and then removed her heels. When was the last time she'd giggled? Then she surged into a run and jumped. She clenched her eyes shut as she collapsed into the crackly softness of thousands of fallen leaves. She came to a stop before reaching the ground and laughed in the depths. Reed shouted and landed in the pile next to her, causing the entire thing to shift. Though leaves obscured him from view, his smile was evident in his tone.

"What do you think?" he asked.

"Can we go again?"

"As many times as you want."

She wiggled her way out, eager to jump again, even higher than before. He followed suit and they saw each other at the same time, both laughing at the hundreds of leaves sticking to their hair and clothes. She pulled some free but he shook his head.

"Don't bother unless you want to stop."

"Never," she said fervently.

He grinned and helped her from the pile. Then they retreated and sprinted toward the pile again. Kate jumped high and twisted, landing on her back. Leaves exploded around her as she collapsed into the pile, and another giggle escaped her lips.

The plume of leaves floated above her, gradually settling on her body until she disappeared from view. She wriggled in delight and shoved the leaves about, but could not reach the ground. She'd landed deeper, so she had to practically swim her way out, spilling leaves onto the ground as she finally extricated herself from the pile.

Reed rolled into view, leaves adorning his body like ornaments on a Christmas tree. She gathered an armful and threw it at him. He was quick to retaliate and leaves flew in bursts of fury.

She laughed and tried to dodge but leaves were everywhere, the now lopsided pile spilling down upon her and engulfing her anew. She escaped and sprinted around the pile, leaping in to knock a section on top of Reed. She tumbled through the mountain of leaves and she heard his muffled laugh.

They fought through the pile and on top of it, taking breaks to launch themselves into the pile in unison. The enormous pile gradually flattened as they pummeled it and played. Their battles were filled with unbridled fury until laughter overcame them, and fatigue finally left them breathless. Lying side by side in the massive pile, she held Reed's hand and watched the stars twinkle above.

"How do you find things like this?" she breathed.

"I never stop looking," he said.

"Even though we're dating?" she asked. "You still want to surprise me?"

He rolled over and scooted through the leaves until he lay inches from her, the leaves a bed that engulfed them both. He reached out and pulled leaves from her hair, his smile infectious.

"So I've won you over?" he asked.

"You know how I feel about you."

227

"Do I?" he asked, scrunching his face up as if in confusion.

She shoved leaves at him again but he didn't take the bait. "You've had me for a long time," she said, her voice turning soft.

He smiled again, and this time her gut tightened, energy crackling up her frame. His gaze never left hers, the light reflecting off his crystal blue eyes, making them look like liquid sapphires.

"You asked me once if I'd keep dating my girlfriend after I was in a relationship," he said.

"I did," she replied, but the moment seemed like ages ago.

"I said I would, but to be honest I wasn't sure. It wasn't until the Festival of Lanterns that I realized the truth."

"And what's that?" she asked.

He was so close she could feel his body against hers, the leaves muffling the contact but unable to remove its power. His lips were just inches from hers and she felt the intense desire to close the gap, but the look in his eyes held her bound.

"I realized that my desire to date you was based on what I felt. The stronger I felt, the more I wanted to see you smile, to surprise you, to be with you."

"And what is it you feel now?" she dared to ask.

The moment seemed to freeze in time. She was highly conscious of the leaves cushioning her body, of the wind rustling the pile, of its chill bite on her face. His fingers were intertwined with hers, an action that had become ordinary but in that moment left her spellbound.

"Kate," he said softly. "I love you."

Light seemed to swell within her chest, spilling into her arms and body as if she would burst from emotion. She wanted to scream for joy but his gaze kept her transfixed, and so her heart shrieked inside the prison of her body.

228

"I love you too," she said, the words the only outlet her emotions seemed to manage.

His smile was the softest she'd ever seen and he leaned into the kiss, the contact bursting the dam of emotions. She kissed him with all the passion her voice could not express, her hands wrapping around his back and pulling him close.

Space was a burden, distance an irritant. She yearned to give herself to him and for an instant thought his physical walls would break. Then his body leaned away and she opened her eyes.

"I want to show you that I love you," she said, her voice husky.

"You don't need to," he replied.

"But I *want* to."

He smiled and caressed her cheek, the touch sending a shiver into her flesh. "It's because I love you that I want to wait."

She swallowed and fought to rein in the desire. Like a ravenous beast it had surged from its cage and yearned to feed, and she felt the hunger. Abruptly he stood and reached down, his hand reaching out to her.

"Would my love like to jump into the leaves again?"

She laughed, the sound tinged with a trace of disappointment as her desire retreated back into its corner. Reed might move slowly, but that just made each barrier they breached all the more powerful.

"She would," she said, taking his hand.

He pulled her up and kissed her again, this time soft and tender. "I've never felt this before," he said.

"Me either," she replied, shivering again.

"Do you want to go?"

He took a step toward the car but she caught his hand and pulled him back. "Do you really love me?" she asked.

"I have for a while," he murmured. "But it wasn't until recently that I realized it."

Her smile could have split her cheeks. Then she grabbed his arm and hooked his leg, tumbling them into the leaf pile together. She would have stayed all night, but the dropping temperature finally drove them from the park. Breathless and elated, she reluctantly sprinted toward the car.

Shivering, she sat in the car waiting for the heat to warm her skin, but the fan kept cutting out. Prepared for the possibility, Reed pulled a blanket from the back seat and handed it to her. Kate wrapped herself against the chill and looked back at the pile as the car backed out of the lot. She watched the now lopsided pile of leaves until a building blocked it from view.

Chapter 6

Kate didn't turn when the window creaked open. A moment later Brittney appeared in her peripheral vision and climbed out onto the roof to join her, settling into a seat at her side. In silence, the two gazed upon the starry night.

Kate had returned home an hour ago but had paced the empty house, unable to contain her emotions. Eventually she climbed out Brittney's window and sat on the roof where she had an unbroken view of the sky.

"You're still in your dress," Brittney said.

"You too," Kate said.

"Sometimes a girl just likes to look pretty." Brittney smoothed the fabric over her knees and then raised an eyebrow to Kate. "I've never seen you smile like that."

"Reed said he loved me."

Saying it out loud sent a shudder of joy coursing through her body and warmed her to her bones. Her smile widened and she glanced at Brittney, who released a long breath and shook her head.

"It's about time."

Kate laughed, the sound reverberating off the back fence in the tiny yard, and she looked to the stars. The heavenly display of twinkling lights was beautiful, but this time it was not what inspired the profound sense of wonder.

She recalled the love she'd had for Jason, but it had been nothing like this. With him she'd enjoyed a sense of companionship and trust, a comfortable love that was easy. With Reed it was like every part of her flesh burst with lightning and yearning. She'd loved Jason, but Reed was her true love.

"Where'd you go after the arena?" Brittney asked.

Kate pointed to the downtown area and described where she'd gone, her smile softening as she told of jumping into the enormous pile of leaves. Brittney remained silent throughout and listened with a strange expression on her face.

"And that's where he told you?"

"At the edge of the pile," Kate said, nodding.

"Do you think it will ever happen for me?"

Brittney's voice was small and Kate turned to find her staring at the roof instead the sky. Her expression stilled the churning joy in Kate's heart and she reached out to her friend, looping her hand through her elbow.

"I didn't think it would happen to me," Kate said.

Brittney shook her head. "How? You're beautiful and strong, and I'm . . . me."

"I didn't think I was either of those things," Kate said. "I didn't realize until after I rejected Jason's proposal, but I had been afraid of a future alone, so I stayed with him because I doubted myself."

"But you're stunning," Brittney said, gesturing to her.

"To some," Kate said. "I'm sure to others I'm hideous."

Brittney snorted in disagreement. "I don't believe that."

"You're beautiful, Brittney, and kind, and thoughtful, and generous. You're real and considerate and gentle, and more than that, you're loyal.

You've helped Ember resolve conflicts and guided me to Reed, all without a word of selfishness. Do you have any idea how unique you are?"

Brittney swallowed and looked away, wiping at the moisture in her eyes. "Guys don't see that. They only see this." She slapped her stomach.

"You *want* them to see that," Kate said.

"Why?" Brittney asked, surprise replacing her bitterness.

"The guys that don't like your outside will never like the inside," Kate said. "And that applies to both of us."

"No one would ever dislike your body," Brittney said.

Kate laughed sourly. "Two years ago I had a guy tell me if I had more to climb he might like the slopes."

"Really?" Brittney exclaimed, aghast.

Kate nodded. "I bet there's another guy on another roof right now, wishing for a girl like you."

Brittney smiled and then her expression turned apologetic. "I'm sorry. I am ruining your night."

"You couldn't do that if you tried," Kate said, bumping her with her shoulder. "But what brought this on?"

"A guy at the dance," Brittney said, and shuddered.

"What did he say?" Kate asked, a flicker of anger edging into her voice.

"He said I would look better naked."

Kate frowned, her anger rising. "Please tell me you sent Ember."

"Worse," Brittney said. "I considered going home with him."

"*Brittney*," Kate groaned. "Guys like that just want sex. I can't even count how many have sent nudes, thinking I would sleep with them."

"You and me both," Ember said, appearing in the window and settling onto Brittney's other side.

"I think we've all been in that boat," Marta said, joining them and sitting next to Kate. "Why do men think that we want to see that?"

"Because they want to see *us* like that," Ember said with a scowl. "Dirty pigs."

"Are you talking about Tanner?" Kate asked.

"Not him," Ember said, her tone softening, "He's nice."

"That's what you say until you dump them," Marta said with a laugh.

"True," Ember said. "But you don't have to worry about Joey anymore."

"Joey?" Brittney asked.

"The dog from the dance," Ember said. "Tanner overheard what he said, and after you left I handled it."

"Ember," Kate said, a warning creeping into her voice, "what did you do?"

"I kicked him," she said mildly. "Once."

"In the crotch," Marta said. "Hard enough he's headed to the hospital. He was crying."

"What a baby," Ember sniffed.

"Is Ember going to be arrested again?" Kate asked.

Marta snorted. "You think he wants to admit a girl half his size took him down? I doubt it."

"You're going to get another restraining order," Brittney said, but there was gratitude in her voice.

"Got to protect my girls," Ember said, looping her arm through Brittney's other arm. "Speaking of which, what happened to you?" she asked Kate.

"Reed took me to jump into a leaf pile," Kate said.

"That's it?"

"It was bigger than our living room," Kate said with a smile.

"What I wouldn't give for a guy like that," Marta said.

"She hasn't said the best part," Brittney said.

They cast her questioning looks and Kate smiled. "He said he loved me."

"*What?*" they asked in unison.

Kate nodded, all the previous excitement returning in a rush, spilling into an unrestrained laugh. "Reed loves me."

"It's about time," Ember said with a nod of satisfaction.

Brittney giggled. "That's what I said."

The four of them laughed together, the sound filling Kate's chest with gratitude. Beneath the twinkling sky she felt a profound sense of peace. She had her sisters, she had her friends, and she had her true love. She was happy.

She was whole.

27 Dates: The Series

The Dating Challenge

The Dating Secret

The Dating Game

The Christmas Date

The Valentine's Date

Author Bio

Originally from Utah, Ben has grown up with a passion for learning. While still young, he practiced various sports, became an Eagle Scout, and taught himself to play the piano. As a teenager he began creative dating and continued the practice into college, where he took a break to do volunteer work in Brazil. After school, he launched his first series, The Chronicles of Lumineia, and has since published over 20 titles across multiple genres. He loves to snowboard, build treehouses, and play board games, especially with his family. His greatest support and inspiration comes from his wonderful wife and six beautiful children. Currently he resides in Missouri while working on his Masters in Professional Writing.

To contact the author, discover more about 27 Dates, or find out about the upcoming sequels, check out his website at 27Dates.com. You can also follow the author on twitter @27Dates or Facebook.